# WOLVES
# IN
# SHEEP'S
# CLOTHING

## READER REVIEW:

"In Wolves In Sheep's Clothing, you are reading about the crimes that involve Pharmaceutical companies, healthcare professionals, the FDA and the FTC and to what end? Money, power and greed that affects the well being of all of us!

Once I opened this book and started reading the first chapter, I could not put it down and wanted to see just how far into the political system this would go. Just how far would a pharmaceutical company go to keep their products on the market? What would happen if a study was released announcing to the world the fact that medicine is being sold and provided to patients unnecessarily without alternative methods being discussed?

The reading grabs you from the first murder and you to find yourself hunting for the hawk-faced man along with the detectives.

The author does a great job with the characters, keeping you involved in the medical mystery and you learn about some alternatives that you could research on your own."

Britt Batchelor, D.C., F.A.S.A., Independence, Mo.

# WOLVES
# IN
# SHEEP'S
# CLOTHING

ROBERT THORNHILL

**BALBOA.**
PRESS
A DIVISION OF HAY HOUSE

COMMISSIONED BY
DR. EDWARD W. PEARSON, MD, ABIHM

Balboa Press books may be ordered through booksellers or by contacting:

Balboa Press
A Division of Hay House
1663 Liberty Drive
Bloomington, IN 47403
www.balboapress.com
1-(877) 407-4847

Because of the dynamic nature of the Internet, any web addresses or
links contained in this book may have changed since publication and
may no longer be valid. The views expressed in this work are solely those
of the author and do not necessarily reflect the views of the publisher,
and the publisher hereby disclaims any responsibility for them.

The author of this book does not dispense medical advice or prescribe the use
of any technique as a form of treatment for physical, emotional, or medical
problems without the advice of a physician, either directly or indirectly. The
intent of the author is only to offer information of a general nature to help
you in your quest for emotional and spiritual well-being. In the event you use
any of the information in this book for yourself, which is your constitutional
right, the author and the publisher assume no responsibility for your actions.

Certain stock imagery © Thinkstock.
Any people depicted in stock imagery provided by Thinkstock are
models, and such images are being used for illustrative purposes only.

ISBN: 978-1-4525-4669-8 (e)
ISBN: 978-1-4525-4670-4 (sc)
ISBN: 978-1-4525-4671-1 (hc)

Library of Congress Control Number: 2012901639

Printed in the United States of America

Balboa Press rev. date: 2/10/2012

# DEDICATION

For many years, it has been my goal to produce a book that that would focus attention on such important topics as nutrition, alternative healthcare practices, the dangers of prescription and non-prescription drugs and the corruption and collusion that exist between our politicians, our governing medical bodies, our very medical educational system and the large pharmaceutical companies.

I have not realized the authorship of this book because I'm a physician, not an author, and while I write extensively on many topics in the health care field, I felt that there was a need for a novel that would capture the imagination and the hearts of its readers and, at the same time, deliver a powerful message.

Through a long time close friend and colleague of mine, Dr. Britt Batchelor, I became acquainted with author, Robert Thornhill, and was captivated by his Lady Justice mystery/comedy series in which he touches on the topics mentioned above.

Bob is an incredibly talented writer who creates books that captivate the readers and truly have that 'I can't put it down' effect. His stories draw you in as you grin ear to ear with his hilarious comedy and suspense as to what will happen on the next page.

As a previous patient, he now has a very firm grasp on health and is enjoying his vitality as he 'works' his way through retirement sharing his gift of laughter along the way.

I have commissioned Robert to write this novel in the hope that many more people will become aware of these important issues. Wolves in Sheep's Clothing is a book that appeals to anyone who appreciates both comedy and suspense, while pulling back the curtain on some our most troubling issues today.

Our failing health and our unsustainable healthcare system (that is truly bankrupting the country) are putting in jeopardy our very future. Our species may very well not survive in harmony with our planet if we stay on this path of consumption and chronic disease.

Luckily, the new direction of humanity is to be Green, Aware, and Sustainable. Reclaiming our natural health is a key aspect to this and a necessity for our survival.

The masses are sick and tired of being sick and tired, of all the drugs and surgeries prescribed in the name of 'normal aging', and of not enjoying our lives as much as we can when we have the balanced physical and mental health and vitality we deserve.

We now know the pharmaceutical and surgery based system is failing us both in our health and our pocketbooks. It's expensive to be sick, and that is exactly how the powers that be like it.

Our bodies, whether by creation or evolution, were not intended to fail us and especially at such young ages.

We have a lifespan of 120 years and a health span of at least 90-100 years. We have been misguided and mis-educated for decades into believing that our bodies fail us at very young ages, that our genetics are at fault and that drugs and surgery have become an unavoidable part of life.

This is absolutely completely untrue.

The New Medicine Foundation became a reality because of the need for a new direction, and a new scientific standard for natural health. Displeased with the current system during my training, I had to search for years for the truth and ability to uncover why we now all get sick and to formulate the methods with which to restore health to our patients quickly and powerfully.

NMF natural healing protocols are actually more effective and tremendously less expensive than those of our failing system.

Bringing this treatment and information to the masses is a key ingredient to restoring humanity to a vital and sustainable path. In short, health is easy to regain when you know how and have proper guidance.

Somewhere along the way of the last few decades, humanity took a wrong turn.

The world now runs on greed and corruption, and the healthcare industry is one of the best (or worst) examples.

Our species is quickly becoming sick, obese and broke!

Fortunately, there is a revolution under foot, and the majority of people are demanding the truth. NMF was created to deliver just that truth in health and healing.

We are now a global and virtually-deliverable healthcare company and are leading the way to a healthy and vibrant future for those who simply want to enjoy this beautiful time on earth again.

This book is helping deliver our message with the enjoyment and laughter of the story of Walt and his mischievous cohorts.

While this is a work of fiction, the story is based in fact.

It is a mystery and who doesn't love a good mystery.

It is filled with humor and who doesn't enjoy a good laugh.

After all, laughter is the best medicine.

It is my hope that you enjoy the novel, but more importantly, I hope that the underlying message will be meaningful in your life and that after reading it you and all those you know will be ready to take the journey with us back to health.

Be Well,

Dr. Edward W Pearson, MD, ABIHM

Over the past several years, we have been looking for a way to send our message of health to the world in a fun and captivating yet educational story and with a style of writing that is savvy and so powerful it may just make you stop and think about your own health choices in life and change them!

This is exactly what Robert Thornhill has done.

Because the practice of life is what we need when we are sick, not the practice of medication, I have dedicated my career to helping dis-ease without the use of drugs.

Chiropractic, organic nutrition and holistic New Medicine far surpass all other choices for my family's healthcare.

As a licensed Doctor of Chiropractic, I deliver true health to all of those around me, pediatric to adult because --- IT WORKS.

My children are not vaccinated and we eat 99% organic. They attend public school and are healthy, happy and vibrant children.

Our family is living proof that if you live a balanced, healthy, organic lifestyle the human body can thrive and adapt.

What about people that don't lead a healthy lifestyle?

When the dreadful day comes that they are smacked right across the face with a diagnosis of diabetes, heart failure, thyroid disease, lupus, MS or even cancer, whom can they turn to for advice on medications and procedures?

What about an Alternative approach?

What about seeking the advice of a Medical Doctor that is Board Certified in Integrative Holistic Medicine --- one who will work side by side in conjunction with your Chiropractor?

There is no other medical specialty I have seen that is trained to think outside of the box, like a Holistic MD. They take the human body and look at the lab work as a whole and heal it from the inside out.

There aren't enough medical physicians like my husband. He is an inspiration. He is a holistic Medical Doctor healing the sick, the tired, and the depressed, by evaluating the laboratory results of blood and saliva holistically. He brings biochemical balance to a body that has been in a state of stress for too long by ordering compounded bio-identical hormones appropriately, vitamins, nutrition, and only using medication when the body is in a state of attack.

Coming from my Chiropractic point of view, the only way to ensure true health is with Chiropractic, organic nutrition, exercise and holistic New Medicine.

I joined forces with the New Medicine Foundation to make a difference and to change the current medical model of healthcare.

If you don't test your levels you just don't know what you are dealing with.

This book ignites a passion within me to bring awareness of just how harmful drugs are.

The first line of defense should be prevention, not the last resort.

Toxins are cumulative in the human body, so be careful what you put on and in the body, especially your children's.

Drugs, medications, vaccines, non-organic foods, environment and stress all lead to illness.

Choose organic when possible, have a Family Chiropractor and stay healthy with New Medicine Foundation guidelines.

In excellent health,

Dr. Julie Pearson, BS, DC

# ACKNOWLEDGMENTS

I would like to thank Kevin Trudeau for his book, *Natural Cures "They" Don't Want You To Know About,* and Dr. David G. Williams for his newsletter, *Alternatives For the Health-Conscious Individual,* which were my inspiration for this work of fiction.

While the names and events in Walt's foray into the pharmaceutical industry and political corruption are fictitious, the story is based in fact and should be of concern to every American citizen.

The quotations cited in this story are taken directly from these publications whose purpose is to enlighten the public as to their health care options.

Walt's skirmishes with the Food and Drug Administration in *Wolves In Sheep's Clothing* are based on actual accounts of raids by the FDA on both a bread manufacturer and the producer of bottled elderberry juice.

You may read more about these incidents at:

http://healthfreedoms.org/2011/06/10/elderberry-juice-drug-raid/ and

http://www.hcgweightloss.com/chapter-4-who-are-they/

Robert and Kay Gordon are the owners of Gordon's Orchard in Osceola, Mo. and the 'Bob Gordon Elderberry' does exist.

For the full story, go to:

http://www.elderberryalliance.org/documents/ByersPatrick.pdf

That such conspiracies exist in real life is something that most of us would choose not to believe, but sometimes, the truth is stranger and even more unbelievable than fiction.

My wife, Peg, and I would also like to thank Mr. Trudeau and Dr. Williams personally, as well as Edward W. Pearson, MD, and his wife, Julie Pearson, DC, and their Wellness Center in Palm Harbor, Florida, and Britton Batchelor, DC, and his Balanced Body Chiropractic office in Independence, Mo., for helping us adopt a healthy lifestyle based on an organic diet, natural supplements and holistic health care.

These professionals have helped us realize that healthy living is a choice available to everyone.

# PROLOGUE

It was nearly five o'clock and Violet Jenkins was in the process of closing the clinic just as she had done for the past seventeen years.

She had just reached into the desk drawer for her key ring when the door opened and a man stepped inside.

He was wearing a business suit and a small fedora on his head. That drew her attention right away. She couldn't remember the last time she had seen a man with a fedora.

Then she noticed his face. Two dark, deep-set eyes stared at her from under the brim of the hat. His face was slender, accented by a long thin nose that reminded her of a bird --- a hawk --- yes, definitely a hawk.

Then she noticed that he was wearing gloves. *"Still a bit warm out for gloves,"* she thought.

"I'm sorry, sir. We were just closing. Dr. Mitchell won't be seeing any more patients today, but I think we can work you in tomorrow."

The hawk-faced man reached inside his jacket and pulled an automatic pistol with a silencer attached.

"Oh, I think Dr. Mitchell will fit me in today. What do you think?"

Violet stared at the gun in disbelief. She was about to cry out when the man held his finger to his lips.

"Let's not make a scene. There's no need to involve anyone else. Now why don't you lock the door and let's visit the good doctor?"

Doctor Martin Mitchell had just hit the 'send' and 'delete' buttons on his laptop when Violet opened the door into his office.

He smiled as his long time nurse and receptionist stepped into the room.

His smile quickly faded when he saw the look of terror in her eyes.

"Violet --- what's wrong? You look scared to death."

The hawk-faced man stepped in behind her. "Actually, Doctor, Violet is a bit upset about my insistence on this late afternoon visit."

"Well, it is late and we close ----." Then he saw the gun. "Look, sir. We don't stock any drugs here and we only keep a small amount of petty cash. You're welcome to it and anything else you want to take. Just, please --- don't hurt anyone."

A condescending smile curled on the man's lips. "Oh I'm not here for drugs or cash and my intent is certainly not to hurt anyone. You have something I want and if you cooperate, I'll just take it and be on my way."

"What could I possibly have that is so important to you?"

The man motioned for Violet to take a seat in the chair across the desk from the doctor. "Don't play coy with me, Dr. Mitchell. You know very well what I want. You have been conducting a clinical test for the past two years and you are about to publish your findings in the *Journal Of The American Medical Association*. I want that study --- all of it."

Dr. Mitchell couldn't believe what he was hearing. "Who sent you? Who do you work for?"

Then it dawned on him. "The drug company sent you, didn't they? A colleague warned me that they would be upset. But to send a thug with a gun ---."

"Thug? Really, Doctor. There's no need for name-calling. Now if you'll just hand over that study we'll be finished here and I'll be on my way."

"I'll do no such thing. You can just go back to those greedy, money hungry bastards in their corporate ivory towers and tell them to kiss my ass!"

"I'm so sorry, Doctor. I had hoped it wouldn't come to this."

Without another word, he turned and leveled the pistol at Violet's forehead and pulled the trigger.

Dr. Mitchell recoiled at the quiet 'pop' from the gun and the dying gasp that slipped from Violet's parted lips.

He watched in horror as blood poured from the dime-sized hole and his old friend slumped forward onto the floor.

The man turned the pistol back to the doctor. "Now that we understand each other, let's try this again. The clinical test --- get it for me NOW!"

The horror on the doctor's face turned into a look of quiet resignation. "I --- I'm sorry. I just can't give it to you."

"Oh really? And why is that?"

"Because it's not here. A colleague persuaded me to keep the study results at another location. He must have suspected something like this would happen."

Frustration and anger filled the man's eyes. "Doctor, I'm rapidly losing my patience."

He moved behind the desk and pushed the chair away. "If it's not here, exactly where is it?"

Mitchell knew that if he revealed where the study was being held another of his friends would be in danger and he sensed that even if he were forthcoming with the information, he would not leave the office alive.

"I --- I don't know," he lied.

"Maybe this will help your memory," the man said.

He pointed the gun at the doctor's kneecap and fired.

Mitchell grimaced in pain and grabbed his bloody leg.

"Now where is that study? Or should we try for another one?"

With every ounce of strength he could muster, the doctor sat straight in his chair and looked the man in the eye. "I'll tell you nothing, you son-of-a bitch. You can go to hell!"

The man could see the conviction in the doctor's eyes and realized it was time to move on.

"Yes, I probably will," he replied. "Maybe I'll see you there."

One more quiet 'pop' filled the office and Dr. Mitchell slumped to the floor.

The man surveyed the office. Even if the clinical study was not here, he had to look and he also had to make it appear that some hoodlum had committed the murders looking for drugs.

Methodically, he opened every drawer and cabinet scattering the contents on the blood soaked carpet.

Finally, satisfied that the study was not there, he grabbed the doctor's laptop and took a final look at the carnage.

Quietly, the hawk-faced man slipped out the door and disappeared into the night.

# CHAPTER 1

Crime in a large metropolitan area like Kansas City never actually stops, but it does ebb and flow like the ocean tides.

Thankfully, we had been experiencing a welcome lull in crimes of a more heinous nature.

Our days had been filled with the usual domestic disturbances, traffic stops and drug busts, but all that was about to change.

My name is Walter Williams and I'm a cop. Actually, I'm a sixty-eight year old cop and still technically a rookie.

I realize that might sound strange, but I started my career in law enforcement at the ripe old age of sixty-five.

In my three years on the force, due to some combination of stubbornness, blind luck and assistance from a Higher Power, Ox, my partner, and I have become the stuff of legends.

In fact, our arrest record is such that we have been dubbed 'The Dynamic Duo'.

The original dynamic duo was, of course, Batman and Robin. Another crime fighting duo that comes to mind is Sergeant Joe Friday and his partner, Officer Frank Smith of the famous *Dragnet* series. There are many more, but you get the picture.

On this particular day however, Ox and I looked like anything but the 'Dynamic Duo'.

We had been cruising midtown for an hour when I heard a distinct rumble. It had emanated from the depths of my partner's two hundred and twenty pound torso.

This, of course, was our cue to pull into the lot of the nearest Krispy Kreme.

Ox had purchased one of those chocolate covered long johns filled with creamy pudding. He had attacked the pastry with such enthusiasm that a big blob of pudding squirted out of the long john's rear end and was leaving a slimy trail down the front of his freshly washed uniform shirt.

Seeing my robust partner cussing and trying to balance his dripping pastry in one hand and wiping the errant blob with the other sent me into a laughing fit, which caused me to spill my hot coffee down the front of my pants.

It was at that moment that the call came from dispatch. "Car 54. What's your 20?"

We looked at each other.

Ox's hands were dripping pudding and mine were wet with coffee.

I grabbed the mike realizing that it would be easier to clean off the coffee than the pudding.

"Car 54. We're at 34th and Broadway."

"Proceed to the Westport Free Clinic in the 800 block of Westport Road. There's been a homicide and you're needed for crowd control."

"Car 54 en route."

I turned to Ox who was wiping the last remnants of the pudding from his shirt.

"Well, partner, it couldn't last forever."

We pulled up in front of the clinic and were met by Officer Dooley.

He took a look at Ox and quipped, "Did you hit the back of a garbage truck on the way over?"

Then he spotted the wet stain on my crotch. "What's the deal, old man? Did you run out of Depends?"

So much for the stuff of legends.

By this time Ox was running short on patience. "Cut the crap, Dooley. What have we got here?"

"Looks like a double homicide. The first patient of the day found the door open and the bodies of Dr. Martin Mitchell and his nurse, Violet Jenkins. They had both been shot. Looks like the place was ransacked. Some crack head probably looking for drugs."

A crowd had started to gather.

Ox grabbed the crime scene tape and started barking orders. "OK, let's get the scene secured. Move those people back away from the clinic. No one goes in or out."

More sirens came blaring around the corner. The Medical Examiner's van and an unmarked car arrived at the same time.

Detective Derek Blaylock stepped out of the sedan. He gave us a nod as he headed for the clinic entrance.

I heard him mutter as he passed. "It's gonna be a long day."

It was indeed a long day. It was after six before the CSI guys released the crime scene and almost seven by the time I pulled up in front of my three-story building on Armour Boulevard.

I had called Maggie to let her know that I would be late.

Maggie is my wife. Actually, we are still kind of newly weds. We've been married five months now.

It's been quite a transition for both of us. Neither of us had been married before so naturally, two old geezers, both set in their ways, had some serious adjusting to do.

I had remodeled the entire third floor of my building into a two bedroom, two-bath apartment with an office.

The second bathroom turned out to be a godsend. I'm not sure our marriage would have survived without it.

We discovered, after moving in, that Mother Nature seemed to call us both at the same time, so I often found myself sitting on throne #2.

I like long hot showers. It turns out that long hot showers fog the vanity mirror preventing Maggie from applying the various pastes and creams that women use. I now shower in bath #2.

I had a walk-in closet built in our new master bedroom. Maggie is a career girl and still very active in real estate. On moving day, her wardrobe filled every nook and cranny of the new closet. My stuff is in the closet of bedroom #2.

I can live with all of that knowing that when it's time to turn the lights out, we will both be tucked in together in bedroom #1.

But even that little bit of heaven required some adjustment.

After a lifetime of sleeping alone, it was quite different to wake up in the middle of the night and hear the deep rhythmic breathing of the person next to you.

I discovered early on that Maggie snores. Not a nasty obnoxious snore, but kind of cute little snorts.

When I lay there listening to her, it gives me a warm comforting feeling knowing my sweetie is there beside me.

One morning I mentioned the snoring thing.

"Maggie, did you know that you snore in your sleep?"

"Oh really?" she replied. "Did you know that you fart?"

I could only hope that if she's lying there awake listening to me pass gas, it gives her the same warm feeling.

Another area of adjustment was centered on my potty training.

Aim, for a guy, has always been a 'hit and miss' situation, so to speak. Normally, I'm a pretty fair marksman, but occasionally, particularly in the dead of night, I will aim Mr. Winky in one direction and he will shoot thirty degrees to the port or starboard. I've never quite figured out why. It's just one of those great mysteries of nature.

If Maggie happens to follow to soon after one of these misfires, I'll hear a "Eeeeewwwww! My foot!"

Then there's the lid thing.

When a guy has lived his entire adult life by himself, there's absolutely no reason to put the lid down. If you think about how many times you pee in a day and multiply that by your age, just think of how much time and energy you've saved by not putting the lid up and down every time.

But being a sensitive husband, I've tried my darndest to keep it down.

Daytime; no problem. Night time; that's another story.

It all depends on my level of consciousness. Fully awake; definitely down. Half awake; probably down. Barely awake; anybody's guess.

If I happen to hear Maggie slip out of bed and head for the potty, I lay there wondering, *"Did I or didn't I?"*

Most of the time, I did, but occasionally, a blood-curdling scream will emanate from the loo, "WAAAAAAALT!"

OK, so I'm not perfect, but I'm trying.

Let's just call it a work in progress.

The biggest adjustment, however, came one night after an evening of popcorn and movies on HBO.

We had watched *Blackhawk Down*, the war story of the Delta Force invasion in Somalia.

I was asleep the minute my head hit the pillow.

Sometime in the wee hours of the morning, I woke up freezing. There was a strong wind in my face and a loud WHAP, WHAP, WHAP, WHAP.

At first I thought I was dreaming and that I was part of that Delta Force invasion with choppers flying all around me.

Then I realized that WHAPing sound was the ceiling fan above our bed going full tilt.

I looked over at Maggie. She was spread eagled across the bed with her nightie pulled up to her chin.

"Maggie!" I screamed. "Are you all right?"

"Hot flash!" was all she could mutter.

It was at that moment that I made a grievous error.

"Hot flash? I thought women your age were past all that."

That night I learned a valuable lesson. Never mess with a woman in the throes of a hormonal surge.

I had seen movies of women in labor cursing their husbands for getting them pregnant.

I now firmly believe the same rules apply equally to both pre and post menopausal episodes.

Needless to say, all the adjusting has been worth it.

I love my feisty little Irish girl with all my heart and she is the joy of my life.

I climbed the stairs to our apartment as quietly as I could. After a long grueling day, the last thing I wanted was to arouse the other four tenants in my building.

My dad and the Professor live in the first floor apartments and Bernice and Jerry live in the second floor apartments.

I love them all but they all love to talk. I just wanted to get home, eat supper and relax with my Sweetie.

I thought I was home free but Jerry popped out of apartment before I could hit the third floor landing.

Jerry is seventy-three years young and has been with us about a year and a half now.

He has become a good friend but he has one really annoying trait: he firmly believes he is the second coming of Rodney Dangerfield.

He lives to tell jokes. Hence, the moniker we bestowed on him, Jerry The Joker.

He nearly drove us nuts with his banter until we turned him on to the amateur night at the local comedy club. Now we only get an occasional gag line when he wants to try out some new material.

"Hey, Walt!"

"Yes, Jerry."

"Ya got a minute?"

"Yes, Jerry."

"You're an old dude. You probably remember Buckwheat from the old Our Gang TV show."

"Yes, Jerry."

"Turns out that Buckwheat recently became a Muslim and changed his name to Kareem Of Wheat."

A pregnant pause.

"Go on."

"Well, Spanky and Alfalfa are really worried about him. They hope he doesn't become a cereal killer!"

"Goodnight, Jerry."
"Goodnight, Walt."

I was just reaching for the knob when the door opened and I saw my sweetie standing there with a frosty glass of Arbor Mist.

She handed me the glass and planted a big kiss on my cheek.

"I know you've had a rough day. Come on in and relax. Your dinner is on the TV tray in front of our easy chair.

Maggie is a wonder.

Most women, especially a woman our age, would have had a conniption fit if their significant other had announced that he wanted to be a cop.

Not Maggie.

She has supported me from the very beginning and, unfortunately, as an innocent bystander, has been dragged into more than one of my crime-fighting escapades.

In my three years on the force, she had been abducted by a psychotic real estate agent, a black drug gang, Hawaiian zealots and a religious nut.

Lesser women would have said, "Hasta la vista, baby" and been long gone.

As we sat, side-by-side in our two-seater recliner, she brought up the double murder.

"I was so sorry to hear about Dr. Mitchell and Violet. It's just all so senseless."

"Did you know them?"

"I've actually been treated by Dr. Mitchell."

"I thought you went to a female doctor."

"I do now. It's just a woman thing. Dr. Mitchell is --- was --- a very good doctor. Do you have any leads?"

"Not really. The detectives are thinking that it was some crack head looking for drugs."

Maggie was deep in thought. "That doesn't make any sense."

"Why not? It happens all the time."

"Because Dr. Mitchell was a holistic physician."

"A what?"

"Although he was a medical doctor, he rarely used prescription drugs. He was a firm believer that the human body was more than capable of healing itself if given a chance. His treatments included herbs and other natural substances. Anything he might have had in his office is available at any health food store. Why would anyone kill two people over stuff that can be bought anywhere?"

"That's a very good question. I'll certainly mention it to Detective Blaylock."

Later that night, I laid awake thinking about what Maggie had said. Maybe drugs weren't the motive after all.

My thoughts were interrupted by a few little snorts from Maggie's side of the bed.

I got that warm fuzzy feeling again, knowing she was there beside me.

I leaned over and kissed her cheek.

Then I rolled back over to my side, farted, and went right to sleep.

# CHAPTER 2

The hawk-faced man sat quietly in the elegant executive office suite of Warren Wescott, Attorney-At-Law.

From his Corinthian leather chair he surveyed the array of photos displayed on the wall behind the massive desk. Wescott with Senator Griffin; Wescott shaking hands with the U.S. Attorney General; Wescott on the golf course with the chairman of the Food and Drug Administration: but most prominently displayed was Wescott with the President of the United States in the Oval Office.

There could be no question; the man was well connected.

He heard a flurry of activity in the reception area. The huge oak door swung open and Warren Wescott strode into the room.

He was a portly man, in his late 50's. His hair was dark with touches of gray at the temples. Drooping jowls that gave him the appearance of a bulldog accented his wide face.

He walked with the swagger of authority fostered by years spent in positions of power.

Without a word of salutation, he stood behind his desk and glared at the hawk-faced man.

"You failed! I sent you to do a job and you come back empty handed."

The man's first impulse was to grab the fat prick by the neck and squeeze the life out of him, but he had played this game before.

"I'm sorry, but the information you wanted was just not there. It seems that the clinical study is being held by a colleague of his."

"And just who might that be?"

"I'm working on it," he said holding up the doctor's laptop. "I'm convinced that he had been emailing the data with this computer. I'll know soon enough."

"And when you find out, I trust the result will be better the next time. Our clients in New York would be greatly disappointed if the findings of that study are made public."

"You can count on that, sir."

"In the meantime, we have another problem."

"What's that, sir?"

"Scarpelli."

"Wasn't Mr. Scarpelli the liaison between your firm and the New York clients?"

"That's correct. Apparently, the greedy bastard wasn't satisfied with two million a year, so he got mixed up with some Columbian thugs and was involved with drugs and prostitution.

"The DEA and FBI were both watching him and raided his house on Ward Parkway last week. They found a kilo of cocaine and two Columbian girls chained in his bedroom.

"They've seized all his assets including the Ward Parkway house."

The hawk-faced man set forward in his chair. "Are the authorities aware of his connection to your New York clients?"

"Not according to my sources in the Attorney General's office. But that's not our main concern at this point."

"Then what?"

"Two things. First, they've got Scarpelli by the balls and he's ready to sing. He's offered to testify against the Columbians and their U.S. contacts in exchange for witness protection. My sources think he's saving the New York stuff to negotiate a better deal.

"Second, Scarpelli has some --- uhhh --- very sensitive files relating to our New York clients hidden somewhere in that Ward Parkway house. Thankfully, they weren't found during the raid."

"Do you want me to locate those documents?"

"Not possible at this time. The FBI has had the house under surveillance since the raid. You couldn't get in without being seen.

"But we do have a job for you."

The hawk-faced man smiled. "Of course. Anything I can do to help."

"If Scarpelli cuts his deal with WITSEC and disappears, we're screwed and so are our New York clients. Scarpelli has to be eliminated."

Westcott leaned across the big desk and handed the man a folded slip of paper.

"Scarpelli's being held in solitary at the Federal Penitentiary in Leavenworth, Kansas. Contact the man I've given you on that paper. He can make Scarpelli disappear."

He took the slip of paper and carefully tucked it in his pocket. "Consider it done."

"Good!" Westcott replied. " The next time we meet I want that clinical study. Do you understand?"

"You'll have it."

When the hawk-faced man was gone, Westcott picked up the phone and barked at his secretary, "Get me New York."

# CHAPTER 3

I awoke refreshed and ready for a new day.

Maggie's side of the bed was empty and I could hear her banging around in the kitchen.

The aroma of fresh-brewed coffee wafted through the door. I hurriedly finished my morning constitutional, pulled on my sweatpants and headed for the kitchen.

I was hoping she had prepared a stack of flapjacks or at least some scrambled eggs, but what I saw on the table was a bowl of white lumpy goo.

"Uhhh, what do we have here?" I queried.

"I thought we'd try something different today," she replied. "It's cream of wheat."

"Muslim cereal killer," I mumbled.

"What?"

"Oh, nothing. It looks delicious."

Then my attention focused on the pile of little pills beside my coffee cup.

This was another facet of our new life together that had required a period of adjustment --- at least on my part.

Maggie has always been health conscious. Me, not so much.

My dietary needs were met by most anything that tasted good at the time, and most of the time that included stuff that was either fried or smothered in gravy.

While I was wolfing down chicken fried steak and mashed potatoes, Maggie would be nibbling on a salad with grilled chicken.

In the first week after we had returned from our honeymoon. I found two brown capsules beside my plate.

She patiently explained that they contained natural ingredients that would promote a healthy prostate.

When I put up a fuss, as she knew I would, she whipped out documentation showing that 80% of men reaching the age of eighty would develop prostate cancer. She said she had waited sixty-seven years for the right man and she'd be damned if she was going to risk losing me when it could be prevented.

I took the pills.

A week or so later, another pill big enough to gag a horse showed up along with my prostate stuff.

"So what's that for?" I had asked.

"That's a one-a-day multi-vitamin. Look, Walt. You just don't eat the right foods. You and Ox are either at Mel's, Denny's or Sonic every day of the week. I won't fuss about that as long as I know you're getting your minimum daily requirements of vitamins and minerals."

Since I wanted to preserve my inalienable right to consume junk food, I dutifully swallowed the big pill.

Another week passed and a new pill appeared.

"OK, what now?"

"That's a probiotic. Your colon will only work properly if it contains the right kind of bacteria. That little pill contains the bacteria you need for a healthy colon."

"So I'm swallowing bacteria?"

"Yes, but it's the good kind."

"Oh, swell."

Then came the vitamin D; then the vitamin C, and some other stuff I can't really identify. But I was assured that it was all natural and all good for me.

As I surveyed the pile of pills by my coffee cup, I was reminded of a story my grandpa told me when I was just a kid.

It was about two country boys. The older one had just cleaned out the bottom of his rabbit hutch. He put the little pellets in a coffee can and took them to his younger brother.

"Here," he said. "Eat these."

"What are dey?" the brother asked.

"Dey's smart pills. You eat 'em, you'll get real smart."

The boy popped a handful in his mouth.

"Eeeeewwww! De's ain't smart pills. Dis is rabbit poop!"

"See! I told you!" the older boy said. "You is gettin' smarter already!"

Maggie was dutifully watching me swallow the pills.

"Any chance these will make me smarter?" I asked.

"What?"

"Never mind."

I guess I should be thankful that she loves me enough to make me take the stuff.

Hey! Maybe I am getting smarter.

A grim-faced Captain Short addressed the squad meeting.

"Gentlemen, our priority today is the double homicide of Dr. Mitchell and his nurse.

"Unfortunately, we don't have much to go on. The lab boys found no fingerprints or other DNA evidence other than that of the victims.

"With the office being torn apart the way it was, our current theory is that it was the work of a junkie looking for drugs that went bad."

I remembered Maggie's statement that Mitchell kept few, if any drugs on the premises and I made a mental note to bring this to the captain's attention after the meeting.

The captain continued. "So far, we have found no witnesses. Our focus today will be to canvass Westport Road and the surrounding neighborhoods. Maybe we'll find someone who saw something out of the ordinary.

"Your assignments are posted. Good luck!"

I held back as the other officers filed out of the squad room. I was about to speak to the captain when I heard the desk clerk call my name.

"Walt, I have a message for you. Sounded important."

I looked at the message slip that the clerk had handed to me. It simply said, " Call Dr. Bart Johnson." The phone number was added.

I guess if someone asked me who my doctor was, it would be Doc Johnson.

Fortunately, I have been blessed with very good health and have seldom required the services of a physician.

I have friends who visit their doctors regularly for check-ups. I know people my age that have colonoscopies every couple of years as regular as clockwork.

I just don't buy it.

I know, I know; an ounce of prevention is worth a pound of cure.

My personal philosophy, however, is that if it ain't broke, don't fix it.

Oh, I've had a physical or two in my life. A nurse takes my temperature and my blood pressure. Then I sit in an ice-cold exam room for thirty minutes in one of those god-awful gowns that open down the back.

Finally, the doctor arrives, snaps on a pair of rubber gloves, coats it with Vaseline and probes the neither parts of my rectum.

Doc Johnson then usually smacks me on the butt and says, "Everything looks fine, Walt. See you in a couple of years."

Sometimes I think maybe I should do more, but then I remember my grandpa. He lived into his nineties, and to my knowledge, he did so without ever having a camera shoved up his butt or down his throat.

All this was going through my mind as I dialed Doc Johnson's number.

Naturally, I was put on hold, but the Doc answered right away.

"Walt, is there any chance you could stop by my office this afternoon?"

"Why? What's wrong?" I stammered. "Am I dying?"

"No, no. This isn't about you. It concerns Dr. Mitchell. I may have some information that will help."

Ox and I canvassed our assigned area with no luck.

There was still an hour before our shift was over so I asked Ox if he wanted to accompany me to Doc Johnson's office. He said, "Sure."

The Doc led us into his private office.

"Martin --- Dr. Mitchell was a personal friend of mine. I've known both of them for years."

"I'm so sorry, Doc," I said. "It's such a tragic loss."

"Walt, I read in the paper that they think it was somebody looking for drugs."

"Well, that's the working theory right now. We really don't have much to go on."

Then I remembered what Maggie said.

"Maggie told me that Dr. Mitchell kept few drugs at his office."

"Hardly any at all," he replied. "It wasn't someone looking for drugs."

"What then?"

"I'm afraid it's a lot more complicated --- frightening, really."

I looked at Ox who had been sitting quietly.

Finally, he spoke. "Please tell us what you know, Doctor."

"It's about a study --- a clinical study that Dr. Mitchell had been conducting for the last two years. They killed him trying to get the results of that study."

"Why would someone kill for a clinical study?"

"Because it's worth twelve billion dollars!"

Ox and I just sat there dumbfounded.

"Twelve billion?" I stammered. "Did they find what they were looking for?"

"They did not."

"How do you know that?" Ox asked.

"Because I know where it is. A colleague of mine was working with Dr. Mitchell. He has it."

"Why hasn't he come forward?"

"He's afraid for his life. If they find out he has the study, they will kill him too."

# CHAPTER 4

Dr. Edgar Pearson's Holistic Wellness Clinic was located in an unassuming brick storefront on Main Street just south of the Country Club Plaza.

It was almost six thirty by the time Ox and I arrived at his office.

We had checked out at the station and I had called Maggie to let her know I would be coming home late.

The office was closed and locked, but as we approached, the door swung open.

A man whose snow-white hair and moustache said he was near sixty, but whose trim and fit body was more like a man twenty years younger greeted us.

He ushered us inside and took a quick look up and down the street before closing and locking the door.

Once inside, he extended his hand. "I'm Dr. Pearson. Thank you so much for coming."

Ox and I introduced ourselves and were led into the doctor's private office.

"I --- I just didn't know who to call --- when I heard the horrible news about Dr. Mitchell. Dr. Johnson said you could be trusted."

"You did the right thing," Ox said. "Doc Johnson told us you might have some insight into the murders."

"More than insight," Pearson said, holding up a USB Flash Drive storage device. "They killed him for this."

"Is that the clinical study that Doc Johnson mentioned?" I asked.

"Yes," he replied. "Martin had been conducting his study for nearly two years and was about to publish the results."

"Why is it here and not at Dr. Mitchell's office?" I asked.

"For the very reason he was murdered. The information on this flash drive is very damaging to some very powerful people. Martin knew it was just a matter of time before someone would be looking for it. Every day, he would email additional data to this office and I would add it to the study. I --- I just didn't believe they would go this far."

"Finally Ox asked the big question. "Exactly who is 'they'?"

"I can't actually tell you who pulled the trigger, but I can tell you who sent the person who did --- Putnam Pharmaceutical Company."

I thought I recognized the name. "They're a pretty big company, aren't they?"

The doctor gave me a wry smile. "Not just big. The medical pharmaceutical industry is the biggest business in the country --- bigger than oil or tobacco --- and Putnam is the biggest fish in the pond."

"So what's so important about this particular study?" Ox asked.

"Have you ever heard of statin drugs?"

I shook my head 'no' while Ox was shaking his head 'yes'.

"Well surely you've heard all the hype on the dangers of high cholesterol --- how it leads to heart disease?"

That I had heard about.

"This 'disease' as defined by the FDA, is the latest scam perpetrated by the FDA and the AMA for the benefit of the big drug companies. Statin drugs were developed to lower cholesterol levels, and boy have they paid off."

"Define 'paid off'," Ox said remembering the figure that Doc Johnson had quoted.

"There are at least a half-dozen labs that have developed statin drugs, but Rolotor by Putnam Pharmaceutical is the biggest. Rolotor alone brings in twelve billion every year."

"Whew!" Ox and I both said at once.

"So what's on this study that is so threatening?" I asked.

"Before you can understand the impact of this study, you need some background in the practice of medicine. You saw my sign outside, 'Holistic'."

"Yes."

"There are two schools of thought in medical treatment. Those who practice as I do believe that the human body was created in such a way, that under the proper conditions and with the proper nutrients, it can resist disease and remain healthy without the use of drugs."

"But aren't you a medical doctor?" I asked.

"Yes, I have a medical degree and I discovered early on that medical doctors are trained to do only two things; prescribe drugs or cut out parts of a person's anatomy."

"But why are you so anti-drug?" I asked. "They obviously work or the FDA wouldn't be approving them and thousands of doctors wouldn't be prescribing them."

"That's exactly my point, officer. The American public has been brainwashed into believing that government agencies are there to protect us and that doctors are gods dispensing magic elixirs that can cure any ill. This is actually the farthest thing from the truth. In reality, they are wolves in sheep's clothing perpetrating one of the biggest scams in our country's history. The sad truth is that every single non-prescription and prescription drug has adverse side effects and should virtually never be taken."

"That's a pretty bold statement," I said.

"Don't take my word for it," he said, picking up a pamphlet titled, *Alternatives For The Health-Conscious Individual* by Dr. David G. Williams. "Here, read this about Crestor, a statin drug by a different pharmaceutical company."

I read the article aloud.

*"Taking Crestor also significantly raised the incidence of diabetes among those taking the drug, which most reports fail to mention.*

*This study also didn't address the findings of other studies where statins have been shown to increase the incidence of memory loss, inability to concentrate, impaired judgement, confusion, disorientation, irrational thinking and other signs of dementia and senility. Statins block the formation of cholesterol, a compound that's essential as an 'insulator' in nerve cells - disrupting the transmission of impulses in the brain itself.*

*This alone should be enough to scare anyone away from taking statins.*

*It has also been well documented that all statins are linked to severe liver and muscle damage."*

"Wow!" I said. "It looks like the cure might be worse than the disease."

"Exactly my point!" Pearson said.

I noticed that Ox had become very quiet and subdued.

I watched as my two hundred and twenty pound partner reached into his pocket and pulled out a packet marked 'Crestor'.

"My doctor said that if I didn't take this stuff that I would be at risk for a heart attack."

Pearson just smiled and shrugged his shoulders.

"OK," I said. "I think I'm understanding the difference in different medical treatments. So how does this study fit into the scheme of things?"

"Holistic practitioners are terrified that literally millions of people, like your partner here, are being prescribed these statins when, first of all, the very premise of high cholesterol being linked to heart disease is under question, and second, the side effects are devastating, and third there are natural ingredients that lower cholesterol at very little cost with no side effects."

"So that's what the study was about?" I asked.

"Yes, it was a controlled study with two groups. The individuals in both groups had high cholesterol.

One group was given Rolotor and the other group was given a regimen of natural ingredients: psyllium husk for fiber, vitamin C, vitamin D and grapefruit."

"What were the results?" Ox asked.

"After two years, both groups had lowered their cholesterol levels, but there was no significant difference between the two groups other than the fact that the control group using the natural ingredients had no side effects while a significant number of the Rolotor group developed liver disease and other cognitive problems that were described in the *Alternatives* article."

"So, bottom line, the natural stuff performed as well as the drug with no damaging side effects and I presume at a fraction of the cost."

"Pennies on the dollar," he replied.

"So if this study is published," Ox said, "It could cost the drug industry billions of dollars of lost revenue."

"Exactly!"

"Sounds like a motive for murder to me," I said. "Who knows you have the study?"

"Just Dr. Mitchell, Doc Johnson and myself. We didn't even tell our staff what we were doing. We tried to take every precaution to protect the exact location of the study. Martin even deleted all the emails after they were sent. We knew there would be repercussions."

"So what do you plan to do with the study?" Ox asked. "I would think you would want it to go public as soon as possible. Maybe an article in the *Kansas City Star.*"

"You boys have a lot to learn about the drug industry. You'll never see a study like this in a major newspaper."

"Why not?" I asked. "This is important. People need to know."

Dr. Pearson picked up the morning issue of the Kansas City Star and turned a few pages. He held up a full-page ad for Januvia, the wonder drug for diabetes. A few pages later there was a full-page ad for Cialis, a cure-all for erectile dysfunction and finally, a full-page ad for Rolotor.

"Pick up any major newspaper any day of the week and this is what you will find. Do you have any idea how much the drug industry pays for print advertising? Millions! Do you think if Putnam Pharmaceutical knew the *Star* was going to print the results of this study, they wouldn't threaten to pull their ads?

"And guess what else? Pharmaceutical companies are publicly traded. I would bet my practice that the owners of most major newspapers are stockholders. To publish a study like this would hit their own personal pockets."

"But what about free speech?" I said.

"Like most Americans, you want to believe that we live in the land of the free and the home of the brave; that our government is there to protect us and that fundamental freedoms like free speech are alive and well. I hate to burst your bubble, but those days are long gone, if they ever really existed. More wolves in sheep's clothing!"

"That's pretty harsh!" I said.

"I've got something I want you to read," he said, reaching for a hardbound book.

It was titled, *Natural Cures "They" Don't Want You To Know About* by Kevin Trudeau.

"Read this and then come back and we'll discuss freedom."

I took the book.

"So what should I do now?" he asked.

"Let's summarize," I said. "You are in possession of a clinical study that could potentially cost the drug industry billions of dollars. The man who conducted the study and his nurse were brutally murdered and somewhere out there is a person who would kill you to keep the study from going public."

Ox looked at me. "Partner, this is way above our pay grade!"

# CHAPTER 5

It was nearly nine o'clock by the time I pulled up in front of my apartment building.

At that hour, nearly all the parking spots were taken so I parked a half block down the street.

As I approached the front steps, I was surprised to see three figures rocking away on the porch swing.

They seemed to be deeply engrossed in conversation and I didn't want to interrupt, so I quietly listened.

I soon discovered it was my dad, Bernice, and Henrietta Krug, an elderly neighbor from down the street.

Eighty-six year old Bernice Crenshaw had occupied one of my units on the second floor for many years. She was a sweet old gal, but it was becoming quite evident that Father Time was taking its toll --- that is until my eighty-seven year old father moved in a year ago.

I hadn't seen my dad in years and one day, out of the blue, I got a call from the Shady Rest Assisted Living

Center informing me that Dad was being evicted for lewd and lascivious behavior. This actually wasn't much of a shock. Dad had been an over-the-road trucker with the proverbial 'girl in every port'.

At first, I was really pissed that Dad had been thrown back in my lap after all these years, but it has turned out quite well.

Dad has mellowed with age and we have developed a bond that was definitely missing during my younger years.

The one thing about Dad that has not diminished with age is his libido. The old goat is as horny as ever.

For better or for worse, his attentions were directed toward Bernice from the moment he laid eyes on her.

Amazingly, Bernice has responded in kind and the two of them have become quite an item.

Post-papa Bernice acts twenty years younger than the pre-papa Bernice. I guess the romance has been good for her.

Their conversation was quite an eye-opener.

"Henrietta," Dad said, "remember the last time we visited and you were telling us that Homer just wasn't --- uhh --- cutting the mustard like he used to?"

"Yes, John," she replied. "I've been meaning to talk to you about that."

"So was he able to get it on with the little pills I gave you?"

"You gave me two of them and now I'm guessing he should have taken them one at a time."

"Oh my God! He took them both at once?"

"Yep, swallowed both of them right before dinner."

Dad and Bernice both spoke at once. "What happened?"

"Everything was going just fine and then, about halfway through dinner he got this wild look in his eyes, pushed all the dishes on the floor and took me right there on the table."

"I'm so sorry," Dad said. "I should have given you better instructions. It's all my fault. At least let me pay for the dishes."

"Oh, don't worry about it, John. We just won't go back to that restaurant again."

That was all I needed to hear. I bounded up onto the porch, said a quick 'hello' and ducked into the foyer.

Maggie met me at the door.

I had hurriedly told her on the phone where Ox and I were going and she was dying to hear what we had discovered.

It took a full hour to fill her in on our conversation with Dr. Pearson.

I had expected her to be as stunned as I was that a large corporation like Putnam could possibly be linked to these horrible murders.

But she wasn't.

I pulled the book Dr. Pearson had given me from my briefcase.

Maggie smiled and said, "Ahh, you have Kevin's book."

"You've read this?" I asked.

"You bet I have. That's why I'm not a bit surprised at what you're telling me. Those bastards would do anything to protect their profits!"

Whoa! This was a side of Maggie I had never seen before.

Then it all started to come together.

Sometimes, no matter how much you think you know about a person, they will surprise the heck out of you.

Now that I thought about it, I don't remember ever seeing Maggie take so much as an aspirin.

I had always been peeved at her shopping habits. I would grab a can of something off the shelf and throw it in the cart. She would pick it up, read the label and say, "Nope. This has high fructose corn syrup. It's poison!"

I would pick out two steaks for the grill and she would exchange them for organic meat at twice the price.

"Why?" I would ask.

She would just smile and say, "Because these aren't laced with growth hormones. They're better for you."

Then there are the little pills by my coffee cup each morning.

So there it was. I had married a health nut!

Maggie could see the wheels turning in my head.

"I'm guessing you're having an epiphany," she said.

"Why haven't we talked about all this stuff before?" I asked.

"Because you weren't ready and I wasn't about to force my beliefs onto you. We're talking about a major lifestyle change here and a person has to want to embrace it or it just won't work."

"Gosh, this almost sounds like a religious conversion," I said.

"You're exactly right. It takes a great deal of faith and commitment to live a healthy life."

"So how long have you --- been this way?" I asked.

"Geesh, Walt. You make it sound like I have an affliction."

"Sorry, I didn't mean for it to sound that way. Let me rephrase my question. At what point in your life did you discover the benefits of healthy living?"

"Thank you. Actually, years before we met I had a friend that had an illness that seemed to defy all her doctor's attempts to diagnose.

"One doctor would suspect one thing and give her medication that didn't help and then another doctor would suspect something different and prescribe a different medication. This went on for several years before she found a holistic physician that accurately diagnosed her original problem, but by that time, she was dying from the side effects of the previous medications."

Then I remembered Dr. Pearson's words; *"Every single non-prescription and prescription drug has adverse side effects and should virtually never be taken."*

Maggie continued. "It was that doctor who gave my friend Kevin's book and she gave it to me before she died. Her ordeal and what I read in that book made a believer out of me."

"Maggie, I'm so sorry. I didn't know."

"I know you didn't and it's OK. Why don't you read the book and then we'll talk some more."

Without another word, she kissed me and left me alone to read.

I picked up Natural Cures and began reading.

In just the first few chapters, I picked up on three very important themes.

The first was the warning that Dr. Pearson had made, that all prescription drugs had adverse side effects.

The second was that all these drugs were unnecessary because, *"There are natural cures for virtually every disease and ailment."*

But it was the third theme that drew my attention. *"These cures are being suppressed and hidden from you by the pharmaceutical industry, the Food and Drug Administration and the Federal Trade Commission as well as other groups."*

*"The health care industry has no incentive for curing disease. If the health care industry cured disease, they would be out of business. Therefore, as unbelievable as it sounds, their goal is to ensure more people get sick and more people need medical treatment. That ensures profits. It's all about the money!"*

That was the recurring theme; it's all about the money; it's all about the money; it's all about the money; follow the money!

That certainly fit the picture that Dr. Pearson had painted for us.

I couldn't put the book down and when I could read no more, I looked at the clock. It was three A.M.

In a few short hours, I would be sitting across from Captain Short sharing this unbelievable story.

He will think I'm a raving lunatic!

# CHAPTER 6

The next morning, after reading Kevin Trudeau's book, I looked at the little pile of pills ---- no ---- herbs, vitamins and supplements, in an entirely different light.

My sweetie, with no fanfare, and in her quiet unassuming way, had been gently steering me into a healthier lifestyle.

While I hadn't violently resisted, I hadn't exactly embraced the idea either.

Maybe it was time to give it a try.

I leaned over and kissed her on the cheek.

"Thanks for caring," I said.

"You're welcome," she replied.

I had thought that the path to an enlightened way of living was not so bad: just eat healthier food and take a few pills each day, but I soon discovered that I had only taken the first few baby steps in my transformation.

One evening we had just polished off a large pepperoni lover's from Pizza Hut. I was wiping the grease off my fingers when Maggie delivered her next salvo in my lifestyle overhaul.

"Walt, we eat entirely too much meat and grease. We need to do a colon cleanse."

"Say what?"

"A colon cleanse. Over the years, especially as we grow older, mucous and fecal material build up in your colon."

I looked at the glom clinging to the bottom of the pizza carton. That thought wasn't how I wanted to finish off my meal.

"There's nothing wrong with my colon."

"Oh really? And just how do you know that?"

"Well, everything I eat seems to come out—eventually."

"Experts say you should clean your colon of mucous, fecal matter, and parasites every year. Have you ever done it?"

"Parasites? What are you talking about?"

"You know, tapeworms, stuff like that."

I looked at a piece of stringy cheese on the side of the box and noticed a queasy feeling in my stomach.

"Is this all really necessary?"

"Let me tell you a story. When Elvis died, they did an autopsy. His colon was filled with over seventy pounds of impacted fecal material—mostly old cheeseburgers and fries."

This was way more information than I wanted to hear about my most cherished idol. "So how does this cleanse thing work?"

She produced a bottle of pills. I guess it was a foregone conclusion that we were both going to be cleansed.

"We just take five of these at bedtime, and in the morning nature will take its course."

Dutifully, I swallowed the pills.

At 6:00 a.m. the next morning, I had a rude awakening. It felt as if a volcano was about to erupt in my lower regions. Fortunately, the bathroom wasn't far, and I waddled toward it with my cheeks clinched shut.

My butt hit the seat just in time, and in the next three minutes everything I had ever eaten from last night's pizza to the hot dogs I ate after my senior prom came pouring out. I staggered from the bathroom, a beaten man.

Maggie greeted me in the kitchen.

"Now doesn't that feel better?"

Actually, it felt like my asshole was on fire, but I smiled and said, "Yes! That was just grand!"

I opened my paper, drank my coffee, and ate my cereal, but before I had finished the comics, the fiber kicked in. I felt another rumbling in my stomach and made a beeline for the bathroom.

I was in the midst of another colon scourge when I heard the phone ring.

"Oh, swell. Here I am pouring out my guts, and I have to share the experience with someone on the line. This day just isn't starting well."

I opened the door just far enough for Maggie to hand me the phone. I thought I heard her cough and mutter, "Oh my God!"

"This is Walt."

"Ox here. I was so excited about what we learned from Dr. Pearson I just couldn't sleep. Can I pick you up a half hour early?"

"Just then, an enormous gas bubble reverberated from the porcelain throne.

"What was that noise?"

"Never mind. Where are you now?"

"I'm actually on the way."

"Give me a few minutes. I'm just --- uhh --- finishing up a project I started last night."

By the time Ox arrived, I thought I had everything under control, but two blocks from the apartment, mother nature struck again.

"Ox! Quick! Pull into that 7-Eleven!"

"What's the emergency?"

"If you don't pull over, we'll be giving our car to Hazmat!"

After one final cleanse, I emerged from the can and saw an elderly gentleman who had been patiently waiting for his turn.

As I was walking away, I heard him mutter, "Good Lord!"

After squad meeting, Ox and I approached the captain and asked for a minute of his time.

That minute turned into hours.

"Ok. What's up guys?" he asked.

I related the entire story beginning with the mysterious call from Doc Johnson, through our interview with Dr. Pearson and ending with the information I had gleaned from Trudeau's book.

The captain had sat quietly throughout my discourse and when I finished, he punched the intercom, "Get Blaylock in here --- on the double."

While we were waiting for Blaylock the captain said, "My, my, you boys have been busy."

Then he turned to Ox. "You're the veteran here. Are you on board with all of this?"

"Yes, sir. I am. In fact ---."

At that moment Detective Derek Blaylock knocked and entered the room.

He looked at the captain and then gave us one of those, 'oh no, not you guys' looks.

"Derek," the captain said, "Walt and Ox have some information about your double homicide I think you should hear. Have a seat."

Blaylock sat and the captain turned to me. "OK, Walt. Let's go over this again."

For the next half hour, I repeated the incredible chain of events that led us to the conclusion that one of the largest and richest corporate conglomerates in the world was behind the murders of Dr. Mitchell and Violet Jenkins.

Blaylock, like the captain, just sat quietly until I was finished.

"Well, this certainly puts a whole new light on things," he finally said.

"When we dug a little deeper into the doctor's practice and realized that few drugs were ever on the premises, we figured the 'crack head looking for a fix' theory was out the window.

"Then we started thinking maybe it might have been a disgruntled patient with a grudge, but all the patients we interviewed seemed to love the guy.

"We were fresh out of motives --- until now. Good work, guys."

That was a rare compliment coming from Blaylock.

"All right," the captain said. "We have a working theory. Now what do we do with it?"

"Well, one thing's for sure," I said. "If our theory is correct then Dr. Pearson is in as much danger as Dr. Mitchell."

"But how would the killer know Dr. Pearson had the study in his possession?" the captain asked.

Then I remembered that Dr. Pearson had said that Mitchell had emailed the new data to him each day.

I turned to Blaylock. "Did the lab boys find a computer of any kind in Mitchell's office?"

"Nope. If we had found a computer, we would have been going through it with a fine tooth comb."

"Then the killer must have taken it and I'll bet that's exactly what he's doing right now."

I explained about the transfer of information. "It's just a matter of time until he figures out who has the study."

"So," Blaylock said. "If this whole mess is about keeping the study quiet, why doesn't Dr. Pearson just publish the damn thing? Then there would be no reason to kill him. The cat would already be out of the bag."

"We discussed that," I said. "Unfortunately, that's just not how the system works."

I explained why no major newspaper would run such a story fearing reprisals from their biggest advertisers and maybe, more importantly, not wanting to diminish their own stock portfolios.

"What about medical or scientific journals?" the captain asked.

"Any study submitted to a journal comes under great scrutiny," I replied. "The methods used in conducting the study, the collection of the data, the selection of the subjects themselves; all this has to be verified. There were only two people who had that information and one of them is dead. If the second one disappears, all that is left is a bunch of unverifiable numbers on a flash drive. So, for Putnam Pharmaceuticals, problem solved."

"So where is this study now?" the captain asked.

"Well, the original is in a wall safe in Dr. Pearson's office."

"Original?" he asked. "You mean there's a copy somewhere?"

"Yes," I said sheepishly, pulling a CD disk from my pocket. "I had the doctor burn me a copy."

"Jesus, Walt!"

Blaylock just shook his head. "You're something else," he muttered.

"I hope you meant that in a good way," I said, handing him the disk.

"What do you know about Putnam?" the captain asked.

"I think I can help there," Ox said. "I couldn't sleep much last night, so I did some computer work.

Putnam's corporate headquarters are in New York, but they have offices scattered throughout North, Central and South America.

"They have eight distinct health care businesses, each with their own corporate structure. One of the divisions, Current Products, is most likely responsible for Rolotor.

"They have the largest research and development program in the world with massive facilities in five states including Missouri and in Europe.

"But I couldn't find any offices in the Kansas City area."

"Shit!" was all Blaylock could say.

"Let's assume for a minute that our hypothesis is correct and Putnam is behind all of this," the captain said. "First, their corporate offices are in New York and we have no jurisdiction there. But even if we did, we couldn't just march into their building and accuse them of murder with what we have now. Their stable of high-priced attorneys would bury us.

"These corporate big-wigs are no dummies. Even if the order to bury this study at any cost came from the top, there would be so many layers of insulation between the ivory tower and the guy who actually pulled the trigger, we could never wade through it all.

"We have to catch the triggerman and work our way up the food chain. It's our only option."

"So, I'm guessing that Dr. Pearson is the bait?" I asked.

"Do you have a better idea?"

I didn't.

"Obviously Dr. Pearson will require round-the-clock protection. Does he have a family? Where does he live?"

"Pearson lives alone with his wife, Katherine," Ox said. "Their children are grown and live out of state. They have a modest home in the Brookside neighborhood."

"Derek," the captain ordered. "You will co-ordinate the protection and surveillance for both the home and the clinic.

"Walt, Ox, I want you on that team. Pearson seems to trust you, so you will be the department's liaison with the doctor and his wife.

"Let's go catch a killer!"

Ox and I went directly to the clinic.

Ox parked in the shade under a big maple tree and began what we knew was going to be a lot of long hours just sitting, watching and waiting while I met with Dr. Pearson during his lunch break.

He was less that enthusiastic about his role as the bait to lure the killer, especially as it affected his wife.

He was somewhat relieved when I told him that officers would be at both his clinic and his home 24/7 for as long as necessary.

Like us, he couldn't come up with a more viable alternative and, thankfully, he realized that when he had agreed to participate in the study with Dr. Mitchell, he was committed for better or for worse.

Once the details of our plan were out of the way, the conversation turned to other topics.

"I wanted to thank you for Trudeau's book," I said. "It was a real eye-opener; especially the part about the toxins we put in our bodies. My wife has been trying to convince me of that for years, but I really wasn't paying much attention."

Pearson smiled. "Yes, you and three hundred million others. To quote Mr. Trudeau, *"Virtually everything you put in your mouth has pesticides, herbicides, antibiotics, growth hormone, genetically altered material or chemical food additives.*

*The same conditions apply in the meat industry. Like farmers and other food producers, the meat industry needs to create a lot of product cheaply and quickly. To that end, the industry uses growth hormones to speed an animals growth, contributing to record levels of obesity and early puberty in our children."*

"Were you aware," he continued, "that over sixty-eight percent of Americans are overweight?"

"It doesn't really surprise me, I guess. So the old saying is true; you are what you eat."

"Let me show you something," he said, opening the door to his reception room. "See that girl in the corner?"

He had indicated a very attractive young lady with a gorgeous figure.

"Yes," I said. "She's a very beautiful girl."

"She's twelve."

He saw the startled look on my face.

"What would you say is most people's favorite piece of chicken?"

"White meat," I said. "Probably the breast."

"Exactly! Have you ever been to a commercial hatchery?"

I shook my head.

"Well if you did, you would probably never eat chicken again. The birds have been genetically altered to produce hens with larger breasts than normal. Their food is laced with growth hormones so that they grow to maturity in a fraction of the time it normally takes and antibiotics because they spend their whole short lives crammed together in such a small space they can barely move.

"Everything that is given to them is stored in their flesh which we, in turn, consume. That's why our children are developing like Sarah out there."

"So are you saying that if I spend too much time with Colonel Sanders, I'll get man-boobs?"

He smiled. "Probably not at your age. But I think you get what I'm driving at."

"Surely the FDA knows what's going on," I said. "Why do they let it continue? I thought their job was to protect the American public."

"For exactly the same reason that Putnam and the other pharmaceutical giants are allowed to poison us with their drugs. Like Trudeu says, "It's all about the money"."

On the way to join Ox on the stakeout, I had a really sick feeling. My Pollyanna attitude about our government had suffered a severe blow.

I had always believed our system was there to protect us and stood for liberty, freedom and justice.

After what I had learned the past two days, I wasn't so sure.

# CHAPTER 7

In his hotel suite high above the Country Club Plaza, the hawk-faced man was studying the laptop computer on the table in front of him.

He was impressed with Dr. Mitchell's precautions. He had deleted every email that had been sent transferring data to his unknown colleague.

What Mitchell didn't understand, was that while the delete key would remove the information from the eyes of the casual observer, it really wasn't gone.

One simply had to know where to look.

He tapped a few more keys and a smile crossed his face.

He had the IP address. Just a few more steps and he would know the identity of his next victim.

Within minutes he had downloaded a full dossier on Dr. Edgar Pearson.

He had demanded a huge fee from Warren Westcott to do his client's dirty work, but he was worth every penny.

With a look of satisfaction, he closed the laptop. His next stop would be the clinic on Main Street.

It was a short drive from his hotel on Main just north of the Plaza, to the clinic, also on Main, a few blocks south of the Plaza.

As he approached, he saw a black and white cruiser in front of the building.

Apparently, Pearson, spooked by the death of his colleague had run to the cops. He had suspected as much.

As he slowly passed the cruiser, he glanced in the window. He smiled when he saw the fat one behind the wheel and the old gray-headed guy riding shotgun. When the time was right, they would be easy to handle.

He continued south on Main, then headed east on 55th to Brookside.

It was easy to spot Pearson's home. A black and white was posted there too.

No problem. Patience was the key. He would wait until the right opportunity presented itself.

In the meantime, he had another chore that had been assigned to him by that fat prick, Westcott.

He opened the slip of paper that Westcott had given him and dialed the number.

After a brief conversation, he turned north toward the freeway and headed to Leavenworth, Kansas.

The United States Penitentiary in Leavenworth, Kansas was the largest maximum-security federal prison in the United States from 1903 until 2005, at which time it was converted to a medium security prison committed to carrying out the judgments of the federal courts.

Vincent Scarpelli was being held there in solitary awaiting the arrival of U.S. Marshals who were to enroll him in the witness protection program in exchange for his testimony against Columbians involved in the drug and sex trade.

Scarpelli was no fool. He was used to living the high life as an attorney in Westcott's law firm and if he had to give up all that to avoid prosecution, he wanted to cut the best deal possible.

He was waiting to hear the deal being offered by the Marshals.

His ace in the hole was Putnam.

Whatever they offered, he was ready to raise the ante by selling out those greedy bastards in New York.

The hawk-faced man was truly impressed as he walked through the long corridors of the prison to the solitary block.

Westcott was indeed well connected. Only a man of great power and influence could arrange for him to roam freely through this fortress dressed as a prison guard.

Passing through the last checkpoint, he signaled the guard to open Scarpelli's cell door.

The door slid open and Scarpelli rose expecting to see the U.S. Marshals.

A sullen look crossed his face when he saw that it was just a prison bull.

The look of disdain became a look of horror as he recognized the face under the guard's hat.

"YOU!" was all he could say before the hawk-faced man covered his mouth and shoved a six-inch blade into his chest.

As his last breath escaped Scapelli's lips, his killer leaned down and cut out his tongue.

*"A fitting end for a stool pigeon,"* he thought as he wiped the blade on Scarpelli's shirt.

He left the cell, signaled the guard to close the door and calmly left the prison the way he had entered.

When the U.S. Marshals arrived later in the day, they found their star witness, stone cold dead.

Warren Westcott looked over his desk at the hawk-faced man.

This wasn't the report he had wanted to hear.

The bad news was that the clinical study was still out there, but at least they knew who had it.

He had every confidence that the hit man could finish the job.

"We have another problem," Westcott said.

The hawk-faced man smiled to himself. *"More problems, more money for me,"* he thought.

"My sources tell me that Scarpelli had a 'safe room' hidden somewhere in that house on Ward Parkway.

"The Feds don't know about it yet, but the idiot may have hidden damaging information there. We can't take a chance that it will be found."

"Would a fire take care of the problem?" the man asked.

"No, we can't risk a fire. Since we don't know the location of the room, we can't be certain it would burn before the fire department arrived."

"Then what?"

"As I mentioned before, the Feds seized the property and it now belongs to the government. With Scarpelli dead, they have no reason to keep holding on to it. I'm sure in the next few weeks they will put it up for sale and you're going to buy it.

"Our clients in New York will provide the funds. All you have to do is pose as a buyer and negotiate a contract with the realtor. After you close, we'll go over the place from top to bottom. Do you think you can handle that?"

"Piece of cake!" he replied.

# CHAPTER 8

It had been a restless night.

I had tossed and turned and my mind just wouldn't shut down.

I was really troubled that the agencies of our government that were created to protect the citizens of our nation, were, according to people like Dr. Pearson, Kevin Trudeau and Dr. David Williams, actually doing just the opposite.

I had known that Lady Justice was blind, but I had always assumed that was just a metaphor. It hurt deeply to think she might actually be turning a blind eye to the greed and manipulations of these mega-corporations.

I was also worried about Dr. Pearson. As far as we knew, the killer had no idea where the data had been transferred.

The killer had taken Mitchell's laptop, but according to Dr. Pearson, Mitchell had immediately deleted every transmission.

I didn't know enough about computers to know if that really was sufficient to protect Pearson's identity.

But I knew somebody who did.

I slipped out of bed early, kissed Maggie on the cheek and whispered that I would pick up some breakfast on the way to the precinct.

I wanted to get to my Three Trails Hotel before Lawrence Wingate left for work.

The Three Trails is the only other property I still own --- mainly because nobody else would have it.

Let's be honest; it's a flophouse. There are twenty sleeping rooms that share four hall baths. If you do the math, you can see some potential problems right there.

I think I would have it bulldozed if I didn't have one final ace up my sleeve, Mary Murphy.

Seventy-two year old Mary is the resident housemother to the twenty misfits who reside there. She's a stout two hundred pounds and she rules the hotel with an iron hand and a thirty-six inch Hillrich & Bradsby baseball bat.

Mary has been with me for years and I think of her as family. In fact, when Maggie and I traveled to Hawaii to be married, Mary tagged along as the Maid Of Honor.

The residents at the hotel are mostly old retired guys trying to survive on seven hundred dollar a month social security checks. My forty-dollar a week rent including all utilities fits right into their budgets.

Others are marginally employable fellows who take day jobs out of the labor pool; except for one guy, Lawrence Wingate.

Lawrence showed up on the hotel steps about six months ago. We could tell right away he wasn't the typical Three Trails resident. He still had all his hair and teeth, there were no tobacco stains on his chin and he wasn't wearing a dirty AC/DC t-shirt.

His story was a sad one.

He had just undergone a triple by-pass surgery. As a precaution, he had given his wife power-of-attorney just in case he didn't make it off the table.

By the time he was out of intensive care, his wife had sold their house and possessions, cleaned out their bank accounts and headed off to Hawaii with a new squeeze.

Poor Lawrence had to start from scratch and at that point in his life, the Three Trails was all he could afford.

Lawrence was a computer geek working for a large insurance company, so I figured he could answer my computer questions as well as anyone.

As I was headed out the front door, I ran into Willie who was just coming from his basement apartment.

Sixty-eight year old Willie Duncan was the maintenance man for the large portfolio of apartments I owned before I retired and became a cop.

Over the years, Willie grew from being just an employee to one of my closest and dearest friends. He lives in a little kitchenette apartment in the basement of my building that I give him rent-free for helping out at the Armour building and the Hotel.

Willie's life as a street hustler before coming to work for me had paid great dividends since I began my career in law enforcement.

His connections on the other side of the law had proven valuable in cracking some major crimes and more than once, my old friend had saved my sorry ass.

It was a no-brainer that he would accompany Mary, Maggie and me to Hawaii as my best man.

"Monin', Mr. Walt. You is sure up early."

"Good morning to you, Willie. Yes, I'm actually heading over to the Three Trails."

"Dat's where I was goin'. Mary has some stuff she wants me to do. Mind if I tag along?"

"Glad to have you."

When we arrived at the hotel two of the older tenants were sitting on the front steps.

They were talking so loud we could hear their conversation from the street.

"Yea, had a pretty rough night. Had the cramps so bad I couldn't sleep. Shoved one o' those suppository things up my arse, but it hadn't worked yet."

The other old guy looked confused and pointed to the side of first guy's head.

"What's that thing sticking out of your ear?" he asked.

The first guy reached up and pulled a big white capsule out of his ear.

"Well damn!" he said. "Now I know what happened to my hearing aid."

Willie shook his head as we walked up the steps. "It jus' keeps gettin' worse an' worse," he mumbled.

We climbed to the second floor and were headed toward Wingate's room when I saw him standing outside bathroom #3.

"Good morning, Lawrence, I said cheerfully.

"Yes, it would be," he replied. "If I could ever get into the bathroom."

"Busy morning, huh?"

"You have no idea."

"I wonder if I could have a moment of your time."

"Why not?" he replied, looking at the locked door. "Looks like I may be here for awhile."

Without using names or the context of our case, I explained what I wanted to know.

"People with a limited knowledge of computers think 'delete' means it's gone forever," Wingate said. "Nothing could be further from the truth.

"To put it in simple terms, think of the computer as the layers of an onion. All 'delete' does is remove the file from the first or topmost layer, but the information is still embedded in the other layers.

"For the more sophisticated user, there are programs you can load onto your computer that are supposed to 'shred' selected files much like a paper shredder, but again, that only removes the next layer of the onion."

"So how does one totally eliminate information they don't want someone else to see?" I asked.

"The only sure-fire way is to totally destroy the hard drive. People getting new computers will often erase sensitive material like passwords to bank accounts and social security numbers thinking they are safe, but if that old computer falls into the wrong hands --- well --- you can see what could happen."

"So, bottom line, a hacker who knew what he was doing could find where a deleted email had been sent?"

"Easy as pie."

Just then, the door to bathroom #3 opened and old man Feeney emerged followed by a stench that would gag a maggot.

Wingate winced and grabbed his nose and as he plunged into the foul depths of #3 I heard him mutter, "If I ever find my ex-wife, I'll strangle the bitch with my bare hands."

I really couldn't say I would blame him.

"Whuweeee!" Willie exclaimed. "Let's get outta here!"

When we hit the first floor landing, Mary was just coming out of her apartment.

Her hair was in curlers and she was wearing one of those big loose muu muu things.

When she saw us her face broke into a big grin.

"My two favorite fellas," she gushed. "I'm just having some toast and coffee. Come on in and join me."

I looked at my watch. "Sorry, Mary. Gotta get to work, but I'm sure Willie would love to join you."

Willie's expression said otherwise and as I walked away, I heard him mutter, "Tanks a bunch!"

The two old guys were still sitting on the porch steps.

I heard the first one say, "I sure wish I knew where I was gonna die."

"Why in the world would you want to know that?" the second guy asked.

"Cause if'n I knew, I wouldn't go there!"

*"If I ever get like that,"* I thought, *"somebody shoot me!"*

# CHAPTER 9

The hawk-faced man knew the value of being patient.

He knew of several men in his line of work whose careers had been cut short by trying to hurry the job.

Several days had passed since his meeting with Westcott and he knew the fat man was getting impatient, but he would just have to wait.

He had driven by both the clinic and the doctor's house at different times each day and had carefully logged in critical information such as shift changes and officers on duty.

He had noted that the clinic was only being watched during business hours --- one eight hour shift --- and it always seemed to be the same two officers, the chubby guy and the old man.

The residence, on the other hand, was guarded around the clock. There were two officers, each on eight-hour shifts.

At four forty-five, he had parked inconspicuously down the block and waited for the usual five o'clock shift change.

At five minutes before the hour a second black and white rolled up behind the first car.

One lone officer stepped out and approached the window of the first car. He saw the window roll down and could imagine their exchange of information.

"How's it going?"

"Everything's quiet. No one's been by."

"Well, I've got it. You guys can take off."

"Thanks, have a good evening."

The hawk-faced man smiled. *"A break at last!"*

This was the first breech in the surveillance team's usual protocol. Only one officer --- maybe a last minute illness --- maybe manpower needed elsewhere on more pressing duties.

It really didn't matter. It was time to act.

The hawk-faced man had waited until darkness had settled over the quiet residential neighborhood.

He knew that the officer's usual routine was to make a sweep of the grounds around eight p.m. and make a personal contact with the doctor before the family retired.

It would have been much easier to take the officer in the yard from the cover of a tree or bush, away from the streetlights, the prying eyes of neighbors or a motorist that might be passing by.

But he also knew that other black and whites made random visits through the neighborhood, and the cop on duty had to be seen in the car.

He watched until the cop returned from his eight o'clock rounds and was settled comfortably in his cruiser.

From a bag on the seat beside him, he pulled a gray moustache and beard, which he meticulously applied to his face.

Next came a matching gray wig, which he slipped on under his fedora.

He checked his equipment, grabbed his prop and stepped out onto the sidewalk.

℞

The officer had just settled in after his rounds when he saw a figure approach. The man was looked like an old-timer and one thing was quite apparent --- he was obviously handicapped.

He walked with a pronounced limp and leaned heavily on his cane.

He watched as the old man approached the cruiser with slow, shuffling steps.

The man tottered off the sidewalk, nearly falling, and the officer seeing him approach the driver's side obligingly rolled down his window.

"Anything I can do to help?" he asked.

"Indeed there is," the hawk-faced man replied as he pressed a taser into the neck of the unsuspecting officer.

The officer's body tensed, his eyes rolled back in his head and he passed into unconsciousness.

Other operatives might have left it at that and proceeded on with their task, but not the hawk-faced man.

The officer had seen his face.

Loose ends --- if you leave too many of them, things unravel.

The glimmer of a blade momentarily reflected in the streetlight before slicing the slumping officer's throat.

He looked up and down the street and seeing no one, slipped into the shadows.

Quietly, he walked the perimeter of the house until he saw what he was looking for.

He slipped a pair of wire cutters from his pocket and cut the phone line.

Soon, this part of his assignment would be over.

# CHAPTER 10

Surveillance is a boring job

Eight hours sitting and watching; bored to tears and yet hoping nothing would happen.

Three days had passed and it had been business as usual at the clinic.

Ox and I had taken turns making sweeps around the perimeter of the clinic and the waiting room just for the opportunity to stretch our legs.

The relative quiet had given us hope that the killer had not learned the identity of Dr. Martin's partner in the clinical study.

But we had to be sure.

After another long day in front of the clinic, I was anxious to get home, have a quiet dinner with my sweetie and just chill out.

After dinner, I poured a glass of Arbor Mist and curled up with Kevin Trudeau's book.

I had been absolutely fascinated with his accounts of government agencies such as the FDA and the FTC. He had provided references in the book and I had spent hours on the computer looking them up.

As I greedily devoured the pages of the book, several passages absolutely stunned me and left me wondering how our democracy had deteriorated to this extent.

*"The FDA has the power to make a new "law". Listen to this very carefully. The FDA has the power to make "laws" and enforce them. It can make "laws" without congressional approval or debate. In order to protect the profits of the drug industry, the FDA passed the most incredibly insane "law" of all time. The FDA has now made as "law" the following statement; "Only a drug can cure, prevent or treat a disease." This is insane."*

I read further that; *"The FDA has set as "law" that there is not, and never will be, a natural remedy that can cure, or prevent, or treat a disease."*

*"Once the FDA has decided with final authority that something is a disease, any company making a claim that an all-natural product could possibly cure or prevent that disease can be legally entered by the FDA unannounced - with federal agents, guns drawn- and seize the natural product."*

"Holy Crap!" Mitchell and Pearson could not only be in the sights of the pharmaceutical giants, but their government lackeys as well.

The passages I had read sounded more like Nazi Germany or Communist Russia than our good old U. S. of A.

I wondered if Lady Justice knew all this was going on?

I read the passages to Maggie for her reaction. She was as shocked as I was.

I was so upset, I needed to talk to someone, and so I decided to call Dr. Pearson. I was sure he was aware of his potential troubles with the government agencies and I wanted his opinion on what I had read.

I looked at the clock. It was just a few minutes past eight --- surely not too late to make the call.

I dialed the doctor's home number and let it ring at least a dozen times --- no answer.

*"I wonder if they stepped out? I'd better check."* I thought.

I dialed dispatch. "Officer Walt Williams, Badge 714. Could you patch me in to the surveillance team at Dr. Pearson's residence, please?"

Minutes passed. "I'm sorry officer, I'm not getting any response from the surveillance team."

"Oh no! Send back-up to that location --- immediately!"

"It may be awhile before anyone's available. There is a hostage situation on the Eastside. Shots fired. All available personnel are responding to that situation."

"Well, get someone there as quick as you can!"

I hung up, grabbed my pants, and quickly explained to Maggie what I was going to do.

"You can't go alone. You have no idea what you might be walking into."

"But there's no one else!"

"At least take Willie."

That made some sense, so I grabbed my old friend and we headed to Brookside.

After cutting the phone line, the hawk-faced man peered into the window.

Dr. Pearson and his wife were watching TV in the living room. A big, black, longhaired Persian cat was curled up on the woman's lap obviously enjoying the loving caresses of his mistress.

*"A perfect picture of domestic tranquility,"* he thought. *"But not for long."*

Everything was just right. The TV noise would cover the sounds of his approach. He would be on them before they had a clue he was there.

He slipped to the back of the house, pulled a set of lock-picks from his pocket and had the door opened in minutes.

As he silently made his way to the TV room, he heard dialogue from the TV show *"Law And Order"*.

*"Law And Order,"* he thought. *"What a joke. The cops in this hick town are idiots."*

He pulled the pistol from his pocket and stepped into the TV room.

Both the doctor and his wife were startled and the black Persian cat leaped from Mrs. Pearson's lap and ran for cover.

"Just sit quietly," he said, "and we'll make this as painless as possible."

The hawk-faced man had two choices; he could just kill them both now and leave or he could try to coax the location of the clinical study from the doctor.

His personal choice would have been to shoot them, but Westcott wanted that study, and if he could get his hands on it, he could see the possibility of a bigger payday.

After he had bound their hands with duct tape, he pointed the gun at Mrs. Pearson's head. "OK, now let's talk."

Willie and I drove across town at breakneck speed.

I was hoping my excessive speed might attract the attention of another officer, but as the old saying goes, "There's never a cop around when you need one."

As we pulled up to the residence, I was relieved to see the black and white sitting by the curb with the officer in the driver's seat.

"Maybe this was a wild goose chase," I said to Willie as we approached the cruiser.

"Don' tink so," Willie said, peering in the window. "Dis guy's been cut."

I nearly wretched when I saw the gaping hole in the officer's throat and the blood soaked car.

I grabbed the mike. "Officer Walt Williams at Dr. Pearson's on Brookside. Officer down. Send backup. I'm going in."

"I'm hopin' you brung your gun," Willie said.

"Oh, crap! My gun!"

"Is you o' is you not a police officer?"

"Well at the time, I was an OFF-DUTY police officer in my pj's," I said indignantly. "I was lucky to get my pants on."

"So wot we gonna do?"

"The first order of business is to see what's going on in there. Then we'll decide."

We crept up to the house and peered into window after window and finally found the drama that was being played out in the TV room.

Dr. Pearson and his wife were seated with their hands bound and an elderly gray-headed guy in a fedora had a gun pointed at the Mrs.' head.

"Dat's an old dude," Willie whispered. "We can take him."

I noticed that the massive front door with an etched glass inset led directly into the TV room.

Anyone standing at the door could see not only the TV room, but down the hall on the opposite side as well.

"Ok, here's the plan," I said. "You go to the front door. His back is to you so he won't see you. Watch for me coming down that hallway. When I give you the signal, bang on the door with your fists, yell "Police! Open Up!" and drop to the floor just in case he decides to shoot. When he turns to see who's at the door, I'll take him down."

"You sho 'bout dat?"

"Do you have a better idea?"

He didn't so we split up.

The back door was unlocked and I found myself in the kitchen.

I looked around for something to use as a weapon. It was dark and I didn't want to rummage around in drawers looking for a knife for fear he would hear me.

In the dim light shining through the window, I saw the stainless steel carafe of a Mr. Coffee. I grabbed it by the handle. If I could get close enough, maybe a blow to the head or a kneecap --- it wasn't great but it was the best I could find.

As I crept down the hall I heard the old man say, "Really, doctor? That study is more important to you than your wife's life? Let's just see."

"No! No!" he replied. "Don't hurt her. I'll tell you."

I could see Willie at the door. We needed to act quickly.

I gave him a hand wave.

He pounded his fist on the door and yelled, "Police! Open dis door you freakin' scumbag!"

It wasn't what I would have said, but it was effective.

He turned and fired a volley of shots shattering the glass in the big entry door. I hoped Willie remembered to duck.

Now that his back was to me, it was time to act. With Mr. Coffee in hand, I charged into the room.

I felt something squishy underfoot and immediately the room was filled with the most bloodcurdling sound I had ever heard.

"MEEEEEOOOOWWWW!"

I had stepped on the tail of a big black Persian cat.

Its screech had startled the Pearsons and the old man as much as me.

He recovered quickly, and seeing me, figured he had better finish the job and get out of there.

I saw him turn and point the pistol at Dr. Pearson's head.

I was too far away to get to him with Mr. Coffee, and without thinking, I stooped, grabbed the cat and pitched it at the old man.

I had never pitched a cat. I had however, seen cat jugglers in the Steve Martin movie, *The Jerk*. I always wondered if that was for real or they were just pulling our leg.

It flew across the room in a big arc much like a delivery in slow-pitch softball.

I had always heard that a cat will always land on its feet and I hoped that would be the case.

The big Persian did an aerial flip like Greg Louganis off the high board.

As he descended with all four legs outstretched and claws bared, he let out another ungodly screech, "MEEEEEOOOOOWWWW!"

He landed squarely on the old man's back and hung on for dear life. The man shrieked and flailed the air trying to dislodge his feline attacker.

He saw me charge at the same time sirens were wailing up the street.

Sensing his dilemma, the old man sprinted away, crashed through the window and sprinted across the lawn with the cat still firmly attached to his backside.

An old man? I didn't think so. More like a ninja.

Willie burst through the shattered door and seeing me standing there with Mr. Coffee still in hand said, "Wot was you goin' to do? Perk him to death?"

It was nearly midnight before the crime scene guys had sorted everything out.

After the Pearson's recovered from their trauma, Dr. Pearson grabbed my hand.

"You saved our lives. If there is ever anything I can do for you. Just ask and it's done."

I didn't know it at the time, but that would come in handy later.

On the way home, Willie said, "Mr. Walt. You 'member some years back, I tole you dat you should try some black pussy?"

I remembered.

"Well, dis wasn't zactly wot I had in mind, but now you can say you has."

What a comedian.

Maggie was beside herself when I finally walked in the door.

"Walt, what in the world happened? I was worried sick."

"I'll tell you," I said. "But you'll never believe it!"

# CHAPTER 11

They were waiting for me in the locker room the next morning.

As soon as I walked in the door, *Cat Scratch Fever* by rocker Ted Nugent blasted from somebody's boombox.

After a few verses, they shut it off and Dooley took center stage.

"I'm happy to announce," he deadpanned, "that the Kansas City Police Department has teamed up with the Humane Society and every officer will be issued a cat.

"When you pick up your cruisers, don't forget to stop by the motor pool and pick up your standard issue litter boxes."

Then, on cue, everyone chanted, "Catman, Catman."

Hoots and hollers all around.

When the hubbub had died down, Ox tapped me on the shoulder. "Well, partner, you had quite a night. Wish I could have been there to help."

"Me too," I said. "Maybe we would have nailed the son-of-a bitch."

Things turned to a more serious note when Captain Short addressed the officers at squad meeting.

"A word of congratulations to Officer Walt Williams. His quick action saved the lives of Dr. and Mrs. Pearson.

"But on a more somber note, we lost one of our own last night.

"This perp is now responsible for at least three deaths that we know of.

"Because of last night's events, we have a bit more information on our unsub; he is a master of disguises and, based on his exit from the Pearson's home, he is quite agile and fleet of foot.

"Until he is caught, the Pearson's lives are still in danger and we will continue our surveillance, but from now on, every shift will have two officers --- no exceptions.

"Be vigilant. Don't let your guard down. We're dealing with a very dangerous man."

Our shift that day thankfully turned out to be like the ones that preceded it; no action, and that was just fine with me.

Last night, it had been after one a.m. before I hit the sack and even then, I tossed and turned before drifting off to sleep.

I kept nodding off in the cruiser, and Ox, bless his heart, would let me doze for a few minutes before gently shaking me awake.

When our shift was mercifully over, I climbed into my car and drove home looking forward to a quiet evening to relax and recuperate.

But it was not to be.

I was heading south on Main when my cell phone rang.

I flipped it open. "Walt here."

It was Dad's voice on the other line. "Where are you, son? I need you! It's Bernice!"

By the time I arrived at my building on Armour, a fire truck, an ambulance and a black and white were parked at the curb with lights flashing.

The sidewalk and the lawn in front were filled with neighbors and passersby gawking for a better look.

I flashed my badge and took the steps to the second floor two at a time.

Paramedics were just wheeling a gurney out of Bernice's apartment.

My old friend was strapped to the gurney with an oxygen mask covering her face and Dad was right by her side.

"Sir, please move aside," a paramedic said to Dad.

I grabbed Dad by the arm and pulled him away so the medics could do their job.

"Dad, what happened?"

"We were just watching TV. The movie was over and Bernice said she needed some water. She got up from her chair and just collapsed --- just fell to the floor. I was so scared."

"I know, Dad. I know," I said as I held him by the arm and helped him down the stairs behind the gurney. "She's a tough old gal. She'll be OK."

I said the words, but in my heart, I wasn't so sure.

After the gurney was loaded into the ambulance, I flashed my badge again to the medic.

"Mind if we ride along?" I asked. "We're the only family she has."

He thought for a minute and finally said, "Sure, hop in."

On the ride to St.Luke's hospital, Dad was right by her side, holding her hand and whispering something in her ear that I couldn't hear.

The ambulance pulled into the emergency entrance to the hospital, lights and siren blaring.

A doctor and two nurses were awaiting our arrival.

As Bernice was whisked away, Dad tried to follow, but one of the nurses held him back.

"I'm sorry sir. We'll take her from here."

"But --- but ---," he stammered.

"The emergency waiting room is through those doors and to your left. You can wait there and as soon as we know something, we'll come get you."

I took Dad by the arm again and led him to the waiting room.

He slumped into a chair and buried his head into his hands.

He sat up and I could see that his face was streaked with tears.

"I can't lose her, son --- just can't --- not now."

I had never seen my dad this way. He had always been the rugged trucker with a Budweiser in one hand and a stogie in the other.

The last thing Mr. Macho would have wanted was for his kid to see him shed a tear.

"I know I didn't do right by you and your mom. She was a wonderful woman and you were a great kid, but I had my head up my ass.

"I've spent the last few years living alone, regretting the stupid things I'd done and wishing I could make it right.

"Then I got the chance to come here and be with you, and I met Bernice. I knew I didn't deserve it, but I'm happier than I've ever been."

His body shuddered and I held his hand.

"Me and Bernice --- we've got somethin' special.

"It's like I got a second chance to do it all over again, only this time do it right. I --- I just can't lose her now."

I didn't know what to say, so I just held his hand.

A tear slipped down my cheek and melded with his on the gray tile floor.

A few minutes later, the door opened and Maggie, Jerry, Willie and the Professor burst into the room.

After everyone had been brought up to date on what we knew at the time, we all settled in for the long wait that we hoped would bring good news.

Everyone sat quietly, silently invoking the presence of their Higher Power. Even Jerry the jokester refrained from his usual inane banter and sat in silent reflection.

After what seemed an eternity, the door opened and a young doctor entered the room.

"The Bernice Crenshaw family?" he asked.

We all stood

"Good news. Ms. Crenshaw is going to be fine."

We all collectively breathed a sigh of relief.

"I'm guessing what happened is that she had been sitting for an extended period of time. She rose too quickly and the blood rushed from her head, causing her to pass out.

"This can happen to anyone, but older folks are especially vulnerable to it. We ran some tests. Her cholesterol is a bit high. We'll get her started on a statin drug to lower her cholesterol and another drug to thin her blood and she will be just fine."

Bells and whistles started going off in my head.

"Just hold on to that thought for a minute," I said to the young intern.

I pulled out my cell phone and dialed the number.

"Hello. Dr. Pearson? This is Walt Williams. Do you remember when you said that if I ever needed anything? Well, I need you right now!"

# CHAPTER 12

An old dude like me can only take so much excitement.

Two nights ago I was hurling cats at a psychotic killer and last night was spent in a hospital waiting room awaiting news on my old friend, Bernice.

Thankfully, all was quiet at the clinic today.

Dad and Bernice had made their appearance early in the day.

Dr. Pearson had given her a complete physical and pronounced her as fit as anyone her age could be. He had given her samples of some natural herbs and supplements and the two of them were off to the health food store to buy more.

When I arrived at the apartment, I was surprised that Maggie was not there. She usually beats me home.

I had just poured my second glass of Arbor Mist and curled up in the recliner when she popped in the door.

"I have some good news and some bad news," she announced.

"The good news is that I have a new listing."

I was dreading the 'bad news' part because that usually involves me.

I was right.

"The bad news is that the house has been vacant. I drove by it on the way home and it gives me the creeps. You're off tomorrow. Would you mind terribly much going with me to get it written up?"

Then she batted her eyelashes and gave me one of her sweet little smiles.

What could I say but 'yes'.

Maggie and I had both worked for Dave Richards at City Wide Realty.

After thirty years, I was ready to hang it up.

Maggie wanted to keep going which proved to be a good thing since I got the wild hair to become a super cop.

Now we are both gainfully occupied in activities that we truly enjoy.

"So how did you come by this listing if you think it's such a creepy place?" I asked.

"Special request from Dave.

"It's really a fascinating story.

"The house belonged to an attorney, Vincent Scarpelli. Apparently, Scarpelli had supplemented his attorney income by becoming involved with some thugs from Columbia, South America.

"They were involved in both drugs and prostitution.

"The FBI and the DEA had been watching him for some time. When they raided his house, they found three kilos of cocaine with a street value of around a quarter million and two young Columbian girls chained to their beds awaiting the arrival of their pimp."

"I've heard it's good to diversify these days," I quipped.

"Very funny, smart-ass!

"Anyway, the Feds scared the bejezzus out of him and convinced him to roll over on the whole organization in exchange for witness protection.

"They were holding him in Leavenworth, waiting for the U.S. Marshals. Someone got to him and cut him open."

"I think I remember reading about that in the paper. So much for protection," I said.

"Would you get serious!

"The Feds had seized all his assets, which they're allowed to do in drug busts, but when he got whacked, they decided to unload the house.

"The Feds referred the listing to City Wide and Dave referred the listing to me."

"I've heard that poop does run downhill," I said.

"What's wrong with you?" she asked.

"Well, it's been a rough three days and this is my second glass," I said holding up the Arbor Mist.

"Oh, good grief," she mumbled, stalking off.

When we pulled up in front of the house on Ward Parkway, I saw immediately what she meant by 'creepy'.

The Feds had obviously not been too concerned with maintenance since they acquired the house.

The grass was uncut and old newspaper and door flyers littered the driveway, porch and steps.

This section of Ward Parkway, just south of the Country Club Plaza was a showcase of stately old homes of varying architectural styles, most of which had been built just after the depression.

This house was Victorian --- no --- more like gothic. Made of brick and stone, it's two stories featured circular turrets that gave it an 'old castle' feel.

The Feds hadn't bothered to put the utilities in their name, so we brought flashlights.

When we stepped inside, we were hit in the face with the 'stale' smell that permeates abandoned homes.

It was not difficult to see that the old house had been a showpiece at one time.

An ornate crystal chandelier hung in the spacious entry and a curved staircase with hand-carved railings spiraled to the second floor.

"Well, we might as well get to it," Maggie said, pulling her notebook and measuring device from her briefcase.

Methodically, we measured every room and Maggie filled page after page with notes.

On the second floor, one of the bedroom doors was sealed with crime scene tape.

We removed the tape and entered.

"This must have been the room where they found the drugs and the girls," I said.

"It's just so tragic," Maggie said. "Just imagine those poor girls --- taken from their families --- chained in this room --- waiting to be ---. It's unforgivable!"

The worst part was the basement.

Like many homes constructed in that era, the foundation was made of stone and over the years moisture had rotted the mortar allowing water to seep in.

A foul, sour smell made our eyes burn.

I had to sweep away cobwebs so that we could get to the furnace, water heater and electrical box.

This was particularly traumatic for me. I hate spiders!

When we had finished, I turned to Maggie, "How are you going to get a buyer with the house in this condition?"

"Not a problem," she said. "The Feds have given me permission to get the place fixed up. I just keep the receipts and they will reimburse me when it's all over."

"So you're going to hire people to clean, mow and repair?"

"Already have."

"When do they start?"

"Today! The utility companies should be here anytime and the repairmen this afternoon."

"So I'm guessing we have to stay here and wait for them."

"Yep."

"When were you going to tell me all this?"

"I just did," she said, smiling.

"So I get to spend my day off sitting in a smelly old house!"

"Something like that."

"That's cheating!" I said. "You are going to owe me big time!"

"Oh, I'll make it worth your while," she said with that 'come hither' look in her eyes.

"Well, in that case, OK," I said.

I wonder if all men are as transparent and easy as me.

I thought I might as well take advantage of the 'owe me' thing.

Since we had been at the vacant house all day, I figured Maggie would be open to eating out and this might be a good time to try to sneak in a meal at Mel's Diner. Since Maggie had been planning our 'healthier' meals, it had been awhile since I'd darkened Mel's doorway.

Reluctantly, Maggie agreed.

I had a chicken fried steak and mashed potatoes smothered in white cream gravy. Yum! It doesn't get much better than this. I can't remember what Maggie had, but whatever it was I'm sure it didn't fit in her diet. We were, after all, at Mel's.

I was enjoying a mug of steaming coffee with a piece of chocolate cream pie when a sharp pain in my back hit me like a bolt of lightning. My arm involuntarily jerked, and I slopped steaming coffee into my lap. That got my attention. I couldn't decide which hurt worse, my back or Mr. Winkie.

"What in the world is wrong with you?" Maggie cried. She's used to my idiosyncrasies, but this was outside the box, even for me.

"Wow! Don't know," I replied. "It felt like someone just hit me in the back with a rubber hose. It's easing up now. I'll be okay." I started drying myself with a napkin. Good thing I had on dark trousers. At my age, someone might mistake my little accident with incontinence.

I had just polished off the pie when the pain in my back intensified and spread around my left side. It would subside and then return with a flourish. Every time it struck again, I would squirm. I finally was squirming so much I was distracting everyone around us.

I paid the check and we headed to the car with me wincing in pain every few steps.

Earlier in the day, Mr. Winkie and I had discussed the possibility of him becoming Mr. Happy, but as we drove home Mr. Back had the final word, and the message to Mr. Winkie was, "No way!"

I spent most of the night pacing the floor in pain. In the morning I dressed and went straight to Doc Johnson's office.

After spending what seemed an eternity in the waiting room, the nurse called me back, took my temperature and blood pressure, and had me stand on the scale. She took the reading and gave me a glance. "It's the chicken fried steak," I muttered.

She asked what had brought me into the office, and I told her of my night's ordeal.

"Here," she said, "go pee in this cup and wait in room three. The doc will be right with you."

First of all, I don't like doctors. Not Doc Johnson though. He's okay. Just doctors and hospitals in general and all those places that smell funny. And I especially don't like peeing in a cup. I don't really know why. When I was a kid, my buddies and I would write our names in the snow and see who could pee the highest and farthest. But somehow that's different than peeing in a cup.

One reason I like Doc Johnson is that he doesn't have the 'God complex' that is the dominant personality trait of many physicians.

He actually has a sense of humor.

I remember one of his comments that endeared him to me: "There's more money being spent on breast implants and Viagra today than on Alzheimer's research. By 2030, there will be a large elderly population with perky boobs and huge erections and absolutely no recollection of what to do with them."

Anyway, I finished and waited in room three. Pretty soon Doc Johnson came in. "Got blood in your urine, Walt," he said. "You might be passing a kidney stone. I'm going to send you across the street for a CT scan. Let's see if we can find the little bugger."

Swell!

I'd heard about these things, and nothing I'd heard had been good. In fact, I didn't know anyone who had said, "Gee, I wish I had a kidney stone!"

So I went to the radiology lab and was escorted into a little room. The nurse said to strip and put on this little gown hanging on the door and someone would come get me. Who invented these gowns, anyway? Why don't they go on like a robe, with the slit in front? And why is there only one tie and it's in the back? You put the thing on and then you have to walk around with your hand clutched behind your back so your butt won't hang out.

Then Nurse Ratchet walked in. Why do all my nurses have to look like her? My hiney did a little pucker as I watched her prepare for my ordeal.

She led me to a room with a sliding table that I was to lie down on. The table would then slowly carry me forward into this giant tube with whirling lights. "This won't hurt a bit," she said.

*Yeah,* I thought, *that's easy for you to say!*

As the table slowly moved me toward that gaping hole, all I could think of was James Bond in *Goldfinger.* He was strapped in a similar machine that was moving him and his privates toward a burning laser.

I closed my eyes and gripped the side of the table. The machine whirred and I disappeared into the depths of the huge cocoon. Lights flashed and as I felt myself being pulled out, I reached down and gave Mr. Winkie a quick pat. It was over, and I still had my privates. What a relief.

I returned to Doc Johnson's office and again waited in room three. The doc came in and said, "Yep, Walt, you're about to give birth to a 4mm kidney stone."

Lucky me.

"So what do I do?" I asked.

"Just drink a lot and pee a lot," he said. "It will naturally come out by itself. I'm going to give you a prescription for an antibiotic. We don't want you getting an infection. And also a pain killer, if you need it."

Great. Painkiller. Just what I wanted to hear.

So I took the prescription to Wally Crumpet, the pharmacist at Watkins Drugstore. I handed Wally the prescription and said, "What's he giving me, Wally?" I can never read what a doctor writes. They must have a special class at pharmacy school to learn to read docwrite.

"Well, it looks like Sepra and naproxen."

"What is it and what does it do?"

"Well, the Sepra is an antibiotic, and Naproxen is Aleve, a painkiller."

"Why didn't he just say Aleve?"

"Most drugs have two names," he said. "Tylenol is acetaminophen, Advil is ibuprofen, and Aleve is naproxen."

Right.

He thought for a moment and with a sly smile said, "I bet you don't know the other name for Viagra?"

I shook my head.

"Mycoxafloppin."

Pharmacist humor.

"Oh," he said, "you'll be needing this too." He whipped out a tea strainer. "Use this to catch the stone. The doctor will want it to have it analyzed."

Great. Now I get to pee in a strainer. That's worse than a cup.

I paid for my prescriptions and returned home.

Willie was sitting on the porch. "Hey, Mr. Walt," he said. "Where you been all day?"

I told him about my physical impairment.

"Oh, Mr. Walt, I knowed a guy had dem stones. Like to damn near killed him. He moaned and groaned for days. Had to pump hisself full of dat Valium stuff to keep from scremin'. When he finally passed 'em, it was like shootin' BBs out his wiener."

*Willie, you're such a comfort.*

I spent the rest of the afternoon and early evening drinking and peeing through a strainer. I had just started a stream when I got the feeling that someone had put a blowtorch to Mr. Winkie.

Then *plop,* there it was. Right there in the strainer. I had given birth to a tiny little piece of gravel. My very own kidney stone. It looked like it might be a girl, so I named it Pebbles. You know, like Fred and Wilma's kid.

# CHAPTER 13

The hawk-faced man was livid.

He had nearly broken his arm trying to reach behind him to apply salve to the deep scratches that the cat had inflicted on his back.

The old gray-haired cop who had been watching the clinic had foiled his plan.

Why had he even come to the house in the first place?

He realized that his mistake had been to try to find that damned study. If he had just killed the doctor and his wife, he would have been gone long before the old cop showed up.

*"Well, that's all water under the bridge,"* he thought.

He had bigger problems. He had to face Westcott.

He knew Westcott would rant and rave and belittle him, and it would take all his self-control not to waste the fat little bastard right there in his office.

But he must bide his time. The payoff for this job was a big one and he would not get paid until it was done.

Patience. Patience.

He would think about taking care of the little prick after all this was over.

As he had suspected, Westcott launched into a ten minute tirade that left him huffing and puffing and red-faced.

The hawk-faced man sat calmly waiting for the attorney to regain his composure.

"We need to get started on the next phase," he said. "Let's see if you can get this right."

The hawk-faced man clinched his fists, but said nothing.

Westcott slid a manila envelope across the desk.

"This is your new identity for the purchase of the Scarpelli house. You are Byron Reese. Everything you need is here: driver's license, social security number and a bank account with fifty thousand dollars. After you negotiate a contract, our clients in New York will deposit sufficient funds to close.

"We have to find that secret room and clean it out before someone else does."

The hawk-faced man took the envelope and rose to leave, feeling Westcott's glaring stare.

This part of the job would be a cinch. Getting to the doctor was another matter altogether.

# CHAPTER 14

I was dead tired after spending the entire day giving birth to my kidney stone.

I tried to watch some TV with Maggie, but nodded off so many times she finally shooed me off to bed.

When I awoke, Maggie's side of the bed was empty --- no wonder --- it was past noon!

When I stumbled into the kitchen, my sweetie had a pot of hot coffee and a stack of French toast waiting for me.

After I had wolfed that down, I decided to take my second cup of coffee to the front porch swing and enjoy the cool fall weather.

Maggie joined me and we sat together, swinging and reading the Sunday newspaper.

Suddenly, it dawned on me. It was quiet.

I couldn't remember the last time I sat on the front porch without being joined by at least one of my building's co-habitants.

"Where is everyone?" I asked.

"I saw them leave earlier," she replied. "I think I heard your dad say they were going to the dollar show over on Broadway."

"Hallelujah," I said. "An actual afternoon of peace and quiet."

But I spoke too soon.

In the distance, I saw Dad, Bernice, Jerry and the Professor strolling down the street, laughing and talking.

So much for peace and quiet.

When Dad saw me on the porch, he said, "Walt, I wish you and Maggie would have been with us. We had a great time."

"What did you see?" I asked.

"*The Bucket List*. You know --- with Jack Nicholson and Morgan Freeman --- the story of two old guys dying of cancer who make a list of things they would like to do before they 'kick the bucket'."

"Sounds kind of morbid," I said.

"Not at all," the Professor replied. "Actually, it was quite uplifting. The notion of being able to fulfill some of your most cherished dreams while you still have time is something everyone should consider."

"It sure made me think," Bernice said. "I thought I was a goner the other night and everyone else did too. But here I am and the more I've thought about it, the more I've decided to make the most of the time I have left."

"Actually," the Professor said, "that's good advice for everyone. Old codgers like us know our days are numbered, but we all know that anyone can go at any time. A wise man once said, "Live every day as if it were your last."

The Professor was right, of course. I thought about the young cop whose throat had been cut and how many times in the past three years I had been on death's doorstep.

"Absolutely!" Jerry said. "We all take life too seriously. I heard about a guy who had saved all his life, bought a cemetery lot and built a huge mausoleum to house his remains for eternity. The poor guy went on a cruise and was lost at sea.

"Best laid plans and all that."

"Well, I'm in," Dad said. "I know there's stuff I want to do before I croak."

"Me, too," Bernice chimed in. "I've always wanted to get a tattoo --- a little butterfly --- right here on my butt," she said pointing to her rear end. "My dirt bag husband said it was a waste of money so I never did."

"A fifty-seven Chevy," Jerry said. "In the movie, Morgan Freeman's dream car was a Shelby Mustang. Mine's a fifty-seven Chevy Bel-Aire Hardtop. The turquoise one --- with lots of chrome --- fuzzy dice hanging from the mirror.

"I was a sophomore in high school. Gerald Gray was two years older than me, and his folks had a lot more money than mine did. He got one. It was gorgeous. I've wanted one ever since."

"How about you, Walt?" Dad said. "What would you put on your bucket list?"

The question took me by surprise. "I --- I --- I don't know. I guess I've never given it much thought."

I looked at Maggie sitting beside me. *"Maybe I should."* I thought.

"I loved that movie." Jerry said. "Got some great material for my act. I cracked up when Nicholson told his young employee that when you get our age you should, *"Never pass up a bathroom; never waste a hard-on and never trust a fart."* That's hilarious!"

"It's great advice," Dad said. "Especially the part about never wasting a hard-on." He winked at Bernice and she giggled.

"Ok, here's the deal," Jerry said. "Let's each work on our bucket list. We'll get back together in a couple of days and compare. Who knows? Maybe we have some of the same stuff we could do together."

Then they started telling 'dead' jokes. It was just too much for me, so I took Maggie's hand and gently led her away.

As the door closed I heard Jerry say, "I had an uncle who read the obituaries every morning. He never understood how people always died in alphabetical order."

# CHAPTER 15

Maggie's crew had done a crackerjack job. The lawn had been freshly cut, bushes trimmed and Consuela, who had cleaned for Maggie many times, had vacuumed and polished every surface in the house.

Now that the utilities were on, the big crystal chandelier in the foyer once again cast its rainbow rays up the beautiful winding stairway.

As soon as Maggie had planted the 'for sale' sign in the yard, the calls started pouring in.

The hundred and fifty thousand price tag that the Feds had insisted upon was a bit high considering the overall condition of the home and most backed away after hearing it.

Maggie called me right after lunch and wanted to know if I had any plans for the evening.

Not having any, I asked her what she had in mind.

She had received a call from a buyer who had driven by the property and he wanted to take a look.

Maggie and I had established a 'no exceptions' rule; she was NEVER to show a vacant house alone and especially to a single man.

Several years ago, three female realtors were abducted, sexually assaulted and killed. Maggie herself had barely escaped with her life.

We vowed at the time that no sale, no matter how large, was worth the risk.

Since I was available to tag along, Maggie set an appointment for six p.m.

When we pulled up in front of the property, a black Mercedes-Benz CL600 Coupe was already there.

"Good sign," Maggie said. "The guy obviously has some bucks."

"Yea, if it's paid for," I said.

Always the realist.

A man stepped out of the Mercedes in a suit that probably cost more than my whole wardrobe.

I figured at that point that the car was probably paid for.

He appeared to be in his late thirties or early forties.

His eyes were deep-set and almost as black as the eyes of those goofy demons on the TV show, *Supernatural*.

His most distinguishing feature, however, was his long, thin nose that kind of curved down at the tip.

As we approached, he extended his hand. "Byron Reese. Thank you so much for agreeing to meet me at this late hour."

I thought I saw a strange look cross his face when he grabbed my hand and looked into my eyes.

Something about him seemed familiar, but I just couldn't place it.

Maggie made the introductions and began the tour of the home.

I had brought a book and a folding chair and discretely retired to a corner of the foyer while Maggie did her magic.

Almost forty-five minutes later, I heard them coming down the curved stairway.

"I think this will do very nicely," he said, "but of course it does need some attention before I could move in. Since I'm new in town, I would appreciate any referrals you could give me for carpenters, decorators and the like."

"Not a problem," Maggie replied. "Over the years, I've developed a huge portfolio of craftsmen that I could recommend."

"Wonderful!" he said. "Then how do we proceed?"

"If you would like to come by the office tomorrow, we could talk about the paperwork.

"Oh, and since you're new in town, do you need a referral for a lending institution?"

"I'm afraid I'm tied up in meetings all day tomorrow and a lending institution won't be necessary. I'll be paying cash.

"Is there any possibility we could start the paperwork this evening?"

Maggie is hardly ever speechless, but she nearly was then.

"Well --- uhhh --- I suppose we could --- if you have time. "Walt, sweetie, would mind running to the car for my laptop?"

I retrieved her laptop and they retired to the kitchen to draft a contract.

They had just left when there was a knock on the door.

I opened the door and a young couple in their late twenties craned their necks inside to gawk at the huge chandelier.

"Hi. We're Paul and Marissa Porter. Are you the realtor?"

"Uhh, no. Actually I'm her husband. She's tied up with another client at the moment."

"We'd love to see the house," they said. "We've been looking at this neighborhood for months and just saw your new sign."

"Hang on," I said. "I'll be right back."

I went to the kitchen where Maggie and Byron Reese were staring at the laptop and explained what had occurred.

"Walt!" Maggie whispered. "I'm kinda busy here. A cash contract with an immediate closing! Do you think maybe you could show them around the house?"

"Sure," I said.

It's not like I hadn't done it a thousand times before.

As we toured the home, my old realtor sense told me that Paul and Marissa were falling in love with it.

When we were finished, Paul said, "It's perfect! Just what we've been looking for. We want to make an offer!"

At that moment, Maggie and Byron Reese entered the foyer.

Maggie was saying, "Congratulations, Mr. Reese. I'm certain that our seller will accept your full price offer with no contingencies. I'll present your offer in the morning and we'll get the title work started."

"Uhhh, not so fast, Maggie," I said. "This is Paul and Marissa Porter. They've taken a look at the home and they, too want to make an offer."

I glanced at Reese and saw a hard look in those dark eyes.

"But I've already bought the property!" he said.

"Well, not exactly," Maggie replied. "You've made an offer; a very good one, but until it has been accepted by the seller, it's still available to other buyers. I'm afraid that's the law."

I saw Reese's jaw clinch, but he remained silent.

Maggie said, "Let me visit with the Porters for a minute. Maybe we can work this out."

Maggie took the Porters into the living room leaving Reese and me in the foyer.

I moved toward the door so that I could hear Maggie and watch Reese at the same time.

"Mr. and Mrs. Porter," Maggie said. "You certainly have the right to make an offer, but to save us all a lot of time, I think you should know that the offer on the table is a very good one."

"We've been looking for just the right house for months and this is it! Marissa's grandmother passed away and left her an inheritance --- a sizeable one. We can pay cash. Mr. Williams told us that the asking price is one hundred and fifty thousand. We'll pay one hundred and sixty!"

*"Oh brother!"* I thought. *"A realtor's dream; two clients bidding against each other. Reese is really going to be pissed!"*

Maggie returned to the foyer. "Mr. Reese, the Porters are exercising their right to make an offer. I'll present both offers to the seller in the morning and we'll go from there."

"How much are they offering?" he asked. "I'll offer more."

"I'm sorry," Maggie said. "I can't discuss the terms of either offer. All I can say is that this is your opportunity to make your best offer, and then it's up to the seller to decide which one to accept. I'll contact you both after the seller has made a decision."

You could see the fire in Reese's eyes. "I'm not getting into a bidding war. I've made my offer. I will be expecting your call."

He stormed out the door.

"Well that was awkward," Paul said. "So how do we do this?"

Maggie spent another hour writing the offer with the Porters.

It was after ten when we turned out the lights and locked the doors.

# CHAPTER 16

The hawk-faced man was enraged.

There was just something about this job that seemed to be snake-bit.

He had never had difficulty completing his assignments, but this time everything was going wrong.

He had killed Dr. Mitchell without securing the study.

He had found Dr. Pearson but that old gray-haired cop had mucked that up.

And what was the old man even doing here?

How could fate have placed the old goat with the very realtor who had listed the house he was to buy?

Everything was going smoothly tonight and then this young couple shows up.

What else could possibly go wrong?

He wasn't about to go back to Westcott having failed again.

He would have to handle it.

He moved the Mercedes to a side street and waited patiently until the young couple left the house and drove away.

He followed them at a discreet distance and watched as they pulled into their garage.

He waited until he saw the lights go out and then he waited a little longer.

Patience. Patience.

Silently, he slipped through the shadows to the back door of the garage. The old Westlock was no challenge and soon he was beneath the car with his tools.

It had to be done just right.

A complete cut through the brake line would drain all the fluid on to the garage floor and be seen.

No, the cut had to perfect; not deep enough to cut through to the fluid, but deep enough so that when brake pressure was applied, the line would burst.

When he was satisfied, he left the garage, locked the door behind him and slipped back into the shadows.

Tomorrow, he would wait for the call that he knew would be coming.

# CHAPTER 17

Maggie couldn't wait to get to the office the next morning.

Two cash offers and the prospect of a ninety-six hundred dollar commission will excite even a seasoned veteran.

My day, on the other hand, was a continuation of the same boring surveillance.

I was relieved when I saw the 'closed' sign on the door.

We followed Dr. Pearson to his home, waved at the residence team and headed back to the precinct.

We had just crossed Linwood when the radio squawked, "Williams? This is Dooley. You out there?"

I picked up the mike. "Williams, here. What's on your mind, Dooley?"

"You might want to come by the Liberty Memorial on your way to the station. Got something here you're gonna want to see."

"Dooley, I'm pooped. I can't possibly think of anything you could have that I would want to see."

"Oh, you'll want to see this. Trust me. In fact, come on over. If you're not glad you came, I'll buy you lunch at Mel's."

"You're on!" I said.

The Liberty Memorial in Penn Valley Park sits on a hill high above Union Station and rises two hundred and seventeen feet in the air.

This monument, built in remembrance of the veterans of World War I is truly a Kansas City treasure.

An elevator takes visitors to the top of the tower where they have an awesome unobstructed view in every direction.

Ox parked in the visitor's lot and we crossed the wide plaza to the base of the monument.

Dooley was standing there with a silly grin on his face.

"These belong to you?" he asked, pointing to two seniors with hands cuffed behind their backs.

When they turned around, I nearly fainted.

"Dad! Bernice! What in the world --- ?"

Dooley couldn't wait to jump in. "Seems these two were going at it hot and heavy up on the observation platform. A tourist saw Lady Godiva here grinding away on Don Juan's lap and called a security guard."

I looked over at Ox and he was trying his best not to bust out laughing.

"Dad!"

"We had all our clothes on --- well --- at least most of them. Bernice got a pair of those crotchless panties and ---"

"No Dad! No details! What were you thinking?"

"Our bucket list. I remembered in the movie Morgan Freeman wanted to see an 'awe inspiring sight'. He got to go to the Himalayas and to the pyramids in Egypt. I knew I could never go there and then I thought of this place."

"I always wanted to have sex in public," Bernice cut in. "My ex was a real stick-in-the-mud, so we never did it. But I'm telling you it was a real hoot!"

"So when we compared our bucket lists," Dad said, "this was a natural. We could kill two birds with one stone. It was great --- up 'till that lady screamed."

"A classic case of 'coitus interruptus'." Dooley said.

With that last comment, Ox lost it. He doubled over laughing.

"Ok, Dooley," I said. "What do we have here?"

"Well, it's obviously a case of indecent exposure and lewd and lascivious behavior. I'd be willing to let it slide and just chalk it up to senility but the lady over there wants to press charges."

I looked at the woman who had been observing with a scowl on her face and her hands on her hips.

"Give me a minute," I said.

With the most contrite attitude I could muster, I told the lady about Bernice's collapse, their viewing of *The Bucket List* and their resolve to fulfill cherished dreams before their demise.

I could see that she was beginning to soften, so when I added a few words about golden years romance, I had her.

It turned out that she was a Jack Nicholson fan, which didn't hurt either.

"Ok, I think we're squared away," I said, pointing to the lady.

She waved and gave Dad and Bernice a wink and a 'thumbs up'.

"Then they're all yours," Dooley said removing the cuffs.

"Have a nice day," he laughed, as he walked away.

Dad took my hand. "Thanks, son. I owe you."

Bernice still had a silly grin on her face.

"Dad, do you think you could keep it in your pants until you get home?"

"Sure, son. But no guarantees after that."

That wasn't exactly the attitude of contrition that I'd been hoping for.

I had just parked in front of my building when I heard the wail of an 'aauuuuga' horn.

I looked in my rear view mirror and a turquoise blue 57 Chevy Bel-Aire convertible, complete with fuzzy dice pulled up behind me.

Jerry was behind the wheel and at first glance, it looked like Don Ho was in the passenger seat.

Jerry jumped out of the car. "Why did I never do this? Why did I wait all these years to drive this fantastic machine?"

"Where did you come up with that?" I asked.

"The internet, of course. Cost me two hundred to rent it for the day, but man, was it worth it."

The Professor climbed out of the passenger side. "What do you think of my new threads?"

"Well, they're certainly colorful," was all I could muster.

"All these years I've been a stuffy old professor. Image to live up to and all that rot. I've never worn anything but stuffy old clothes; brown tweed suits; ugly ties and cardigan sweaters.

"I've always wanted a wild colorful shirt that shouted to the world, 'I'm not a stuffy old guy.'"

I looked at the aloha shirt complete with pineapples, surfboards, palm trees and hula girls.

"Well, that one certainly does shout."

"Let's go get Willie and take him for a spin," Jerry said, grabbing the Professor's arm.

Off they trotted like a couple of high school kids.

The bucket list.

After today's events I didn't know whether to love it or hate it.

It had been a long day. I was happy to get home.

Maggie had had a light day at the real estate office, and when I walked in the door she was busy bustling around the kitchen.

She handed me a glass of Arbor Mist and basically told me to get lost. Since she was home early, she had decided to make us something special for supper.

That's not always a good sign.

While I love Maggie dearly, I didn't marry her for her culinary skills. She had been a career woman all her life, and I'm willing to bet that over the years she had eaten more meals out than she had prepared at home.

With glass in hand, I was headed out the kitchen door when I spotted the open cookbook. The title was Dr. Don's Organic Cookbook. Immediately, my mind was flooded with thoughts of tofu, seaweed, and other gastronomical unmentionables.

"Maggie! Are you sure I can't take you out for dinner?"

"No, silly. I've been working all afternoon on this meal. You'll love it! It's something new you've never had before."

"I'll bet that's right," I mumbled as she pushed me out the door.

I had grabbed the paper on my way out and was just finishing the sports section when I heard her announce, "Supper's ready!"

Reluctantly, I climbed the stairs. I was starving, but I dreaded what might be waiting for me on the table. I opened the door, and the intoxicating aroma of meat filled my nostrils.

*Hmm, that certainly doesn't smell like seaweed.*

I sat down at the table, and Maggie placed a sizzling hunk of something that resembled Alpo in a can on the table.

"Ta-da!" she said proudly.

"Gee, that's really—uh—unusual. What exactly is it?"

"Meatloaf, silly."

"Really?"

"Yes, it's made of ground turkey, ground beef, eggs, spices, and a whole bunch of other stuff. And it's all organic!"

"I guess that's good?"

"Of course! No pesticides, no hormones. It's all natural."

Natural wasn't exactly the adjective I had in mind. Maggie watched anxiously as I scooped the first bite onto my fork. I had prepared myself to stifle my gag reflex, but to my surprise, it tasted wonderful. I shoveled in a second bite just to make sure.

"Maggie! This is actually good!"

"You don't have to sound so surprised."

"Oh, sorry. So this stuff is really healthful?"

"It's a whole lot healthier than greasy pizza, cheeseburgers, and fries."

"So if I eat this stuff all the time I can get out of cleansing my colon—maybe forever?"

"Don't push your luck!"

# CHAPTER 18

Ox and I were on our lunch break when I got the call from Maggie.

"Walt, you're never going to believe what happened this morning!"

"I'll bite. What?"

"I called the sellers and presented the two cash offers on the Ward Parkway house. Naturally, they accepted the higher bid from the young couple.

"They were so thrilled when I told them their offer had been accepted. I made an appointment at ten for them to come in and complete the paperwork.

"Then I called Byron Reese. I figured that he'd have a cow. He seemed so upset last night. But he didn't. He said he guessed it just wasn't meant to be."

"That is an odd reaction," I said. "He was ready to chew nails last night."

"Anyway," she continued, "I asked if he wanted to be in a back-up position so that he would have first chance at the home if anything fell through. He said, "Sure," Then he wanted to know if I could show him other homes."

"That's odd too," I said. "Most buyers would have been so upset with the realtor, they would have moved on."

"Well, all that's not the weird part."

"There's more?"

"I'll say there is. The Porter's didn't show up for their ten o'clock appointment. I called their cell and a police officer picked up.

"It seems that the Porter's were on their way to the office and rear-ended a tractor-trailer on the Broadway Bridge.

"Walt, they're both dead!"

I was stunned.

I knew stuff like that could happen. I had a buyer once that failed to show up for his closing. I tried and tried to reach him with no luck. The next morning, I saw his picture in the *Kansas City Star*. He had been mugged and murdered the day before.

"So don't tell me," I said. "You called Byron Reese and told him he was in the driver's seat."

"Yes. He said that he was sad for the kids, but maybe it was just meant to be after all."

"Very convenient," I said. "I'm wondering if that could be why he wasn't upset this morning when you told him he wasn't getting the house."

"Walt! Surely you don't think --- I mean --- not just to buy a house?"

"Who knows? You know how I feel about coincidences --- there just aren't that many. I'll talk to the officers on the scene and see what I can find out."

"Well, talk quick. Reese wants to close as soon as possible and I've set up inspections for five o'clock this afternoon."

"I'll be there!"

By three o'clock, the Porter's car had been towed to the storage lot. I found the officer who had filed the report.

"Any idea what caused the accident?" I asked.

"Looks like brake failure."

"Did anything about the brakes look suspicious?"

"You mean like was the brake line cut? Nope. That was the first thing they checked. The line did have a worn spot, but it looks like a rupture all the way."

"So, there's no way the brakes could have been tampered with?"

"I guess you could never rule that out, but if someone did, they were damn good. Why all the questions? Is there something we should be looking at?"

"I guess not. It's just that the Porter's were on their way to see Maggie to buy a house. I told her I'd check."

"That's rough," he said. "Sorry to hear it."

When I pulled up in front of the Ward Parkway house, there were already four vehicles parked on the street.

In addition to Maggie's car and Reese's Mercedes, there were the commercial vehicles of our two old friends.

Maggie and I had used Jake The Bugman and John Krantz's Hometown Inspection services for many years.

Jake is a crusty old guy with a great sense of humor. He even dressed up as a girl once for a realtor function. You gotta love a guy like that. He's stout, but not fat and in pretty good shape for a guy approaching sixty. I've always loved his Bugman motto, *"If it flies, it dies. If it crawls, it falls."*

John is a bit older and a bit more portly, but as sweet a guy as you will ever see. His job is to uncover any flaws or latent defects in a house and report them to the prospective buyer. The reason we have always used John is that he could be completely honest with a buyer without scaring them away. I guess if he was a doctor, you could say he had a great bedside manner.

Maggie had just completed the introductions when I entered the foyer.

Jake's job was to look for termites, but I noticed that he had his pressure sprayer with him today, which was unusual.

"What's with the sprayer?" I asked.

Maggie jumped in. "I asked him to bring it. The house has been closed up for awhile and I've seen some creepy, crawly things, so I'm paying for a treatment as a thank-you gift to Mr. Reese."

"I appreciate that very much," Reese responded.

"I think I'll start in the basement," Jake said.

"I'll go with you," John replied. "Maybe you can zap some of those spiders before I go crawling around."

"How long will this all take?" Reese asked.

"Oh, a house this size --- probably an hour and a half --- maybe two depending on what I find."

"If you all don't mind," Reese said, "I'm going to look through the house on my own. I need to make some notes regarding the renovation."

Maggie had some computer work to do, so I tagged along with the inspectors.

The house's old stone foundation was porous enough that recent rains had seeped into the basement and stood in stagnant puddles on the floor.

Jake was first down the stairs and I heard him exclaim, "Wheeeew! Smells like ass-crack down here."

"I'll note that in my report," John said. "How do you spell ass-crack?"

Thankfully, the buyer was out of earshot.

I watched the guys do their thing for a while and when Jake started spraying the insecticide, I figured it was time to beat a hasty retreat.

Maggie was still at her computer, so I retrieved my book from the car and read.

After about an hour, the guys showed up in the kitchen.

"I found something strange," John said. "All the circuits in the electrical box are marked except one. It's hot, but I can't seem to find where it goes.

"Jake has been helping me trace the line, but we've come to a dead end. It seems to go to the garage, but all of the circuits there are accounted for.

"Would you and Maggie want to take a look?"

We all headed for the garage.

Everything looked just like a garage is supposed to. It was a double car about twenty feet wide. There were storage shelves along each side and a large cabinet mounted on the back wall.

Then I remembered coming into the garage from the kitchen area and something about the dimensions didn't seem quite right.

I opened the garage door and went around to the side and back of the house and mentally calculated the outside dimensions.

When I returned, I started tapping on the back garage wall.

"From the outside, it looks like there's maybe twelve feet of space we're not seeing in here. There has to be something behind this wall."

We all tapped and poked and sure enough, it sounded hollow.

I opened the cabinet on the back wall. It looked like any garage storage cabinet. There were pegs where tools had obviously hung.

I tapped and poked around the cabinet and then started twisting and pulling the pegs.

Suddenly, there was a 'CLICK' and the cabinet became a door.

We all stared in silence into the darkness of the hidden room.

Jake was the first to act. He flipped on his flashlight and found a light switch.

"Well, here's your missing circuit," he said.

When the lights came on, we just stood frozen.

The room was twelve feet deep and the width of the garage. There were four twin beds, each one equipped with manacles and chains. A porta-potty was in one corner.

"This must have been where Scarpelli kept the poor girls they were importing as sex slaves," I said.

Then on a small table, I saw a package about the size of a brick.

"And I'll bet that's another kilo of cocaine.

"Stay out here, all of you. I need to call this in."

I reached for my phone. "Damn! I left my phone by my chair in the kitchen. I'll be right back."

I hurried back to the kitchen and found my phone.

Just before I reached the door to the garage, I heard a voice, "All of you. Just stay right where you are. Thank you so much for your good work. You saved me a lot of time and effort locating this room."

I peeked around the doorframe and saw Byron Reese with a gun pointed at Maggie and my two friends.

"So sorry that it had to end this way for you," Reese said. "Once I clean out the evidence, it may be years before they find your bodies in this hidden room. Well, maybe not. I'm sure there will be quite an odor."

I slipped back into the kitchen looking for a weapon --- anything that I could use, but like Mother Hubbard, found the cupboards bare.

Then I saw Jake's sprayer filled with insecticide.

I had seen Jake pump up the sprayer and shoot a stream a good ten feet into rafters and eves.

*"Seems appropriate,"* I thought. *"This stuff is designed to kill vermin of all kinds and Reese certainly fills the bill."*

I did a quick mental calculation. There were three of us, a combined six hundred pounds and hundred and eighty years of experience against one guy. If I could momentarily blind him, we ought to be able to take him.

I quietly pumped the sprayer and crept back to the garage entrance just in time to hear Reese say, "Wait a minute. Where's the old guy?"

"Right here, asshole," I shouted. "Take this!"

I shot a stream of insecticide that hit him squarely in the face.

When his hands went up to his eyes, Jake saw an opening and hit him like a linebacker. The gun flew away and John and I moved in for the kill.

What happened next was surreal.

My charge was met with a foot in my solar plexus. John took a chop across the throat and Jake screamed as Reese landed a punch in the kidney.

I had seen Bruce Lee movies where the little ninja guy would take down a whole pack of ruffians, but I figured that was just Hollywood.

Apparently not!

With the three of us writhing in pain on the garage floor, Reese rubbed his burning eyes and looked for his gun.

Fortunately, during the time it took to get our asses handed to us on a platter, Maggie had picked up the gun and was holding it in shaking hands.

"Shoot!" I screamed. "Shoot!"

I could see Maggie struggling with the trigger with no result. The safety must have been on.

Reese must have decided to get the hell out before Maggie could find the safety. When he turned and ran, I recognized the loping gait. It was the same guy who had killed the cop and tried to kill the Pearsons.

Byron Reese was our guy!

Fortunately, none of us was seriously injured.

When the pain had subsided, Jake said to John, "I'm guessing we probably won't be getting paid for these inspections."

I called the station and reported what had occurred.

While we waited for Blaylock and the CSI team, I carefully looked around the hidden room.

I found a metal box in a metal file cabinet along the back wall.

I examined the contents and what I read took my breath away.

Scarpelli wasn't killed by Columbians.

He was killed by a group far more frightening

And I knew who they were!

# CHAPTER 19

When I had seen what was in the metal file cabinet, everything started to make sense.

It was all about the study.

Dr. Mitchell, a holistic physician, had conducted a two-year study on cholesterol, comparing a regimen of natural ingredients with the drug, Rolotor, produced by Putnam Pharmaceuticals.

Mitchell's study revealed that the natural ingredients were as effective in lowering cholesterol as the drug without the dangerous side effects.

If the study was released, it could cost Putnam and other pharmaceutical giants who had similar drugs, billions of dollars.

Reese, or whatever the guy's real name was, killed Mitchell and his assistant, Violet Jenkins to obtain the study.

Reese figured out that Dr. Pearson had the study, and he and his wife would have been killed along with the officer who had been watching the house if I hadn't happened by.

Up until now, Scarpelli's death had not been connected to the study in any way until the contents of the hidden room were found.

Scarpelli was an attorney with a huge law firm owned by Warren Westcott.

According to the information in the metal box, Putnam Pharmaceuticals was one of Westcott's biggest clients.

Scarpelli got greedy and started moonlighting with the Columbians, which got the attention of the Feds.

When Scarpelli was busted and opted for witness protection, the powerful men named in the metal box, couldn't take the chance that Scarpelli would use his information to cut a better deal, so they had him killed.

They knew about the incriminating evidence in the hidden room, but couldn't get access to the house without getting caught, so they hired Reese to buy the house so they could tear it apart.

Now, the Porters, an innocent young couple, were dead, and I'd bet anything that it wasn't an accident.

Having seen the names in the metal box, I returned to some passages I had read in Kevin Trudeau's book.

They certainly made more sense now.

*"--- the FDA is the agency that approves drugs. And when a company gets a drug approved, it's like putting billions of dollars of profits in the bank. So companies will do anything to get the FDA to approve drugs. It's interesting to note that of the last twenty FDA commissioners, twelve of them went to work directly for the drug industry upon leaving the FDA and were paid millions of dollars."*

That certainly accounted for one name I saw in the box.

*"Would it surprise you that many members of the FDA and FTC own stock in drug companies? Would it surprise you that many members of congress own stock in drug companies? Would it surprise you that members of the news media that are supposed to be impartially presenting news own stock in drug companies?"*

That statement accounted for several other prominent names I had seen.

All wolves in sheep's clothing!

But the one statement that Trudeau kept hammering was *"It's all about the money. It's always about the money."*

When I spoke with Captain Short about the contents of the metal box, his comment was, "Walt, this is bigger than we can handle. I'm going to have to get the FBI involved."

He scheduled an appointment for the next morning for us to meet with the Feds.

When I arrived, the Captain greeted me.

"Walt, I think you know these gentlemen, agents Blackburn, Finch, Greely and Barnes."

I knew them all right. We had actually worked two cases together.

The first one involved the kidnapping of the owner of some very valuable Elvis tapes. They had totally botched the job. But Willie, my old friend, and Maxine, a hooker friend of his, had saved the day.

The second had better results. A group of religious zealots were bent on blowing up sin-riddled Kansas

City and had abducted Maggie and Willie to force me to help them accomplish their goals. Fortunately, the Fed's plan had succeeded and we parted on good terms.

"The agents have some tape they would like you to look at," the Captain said.

Blackburn flipped open a laptop, punched a few keys and a grainy tape began to play.

I could tell it was in some kind of jail facility.

Presently, a figure in a guard's uniform appeared. I looked closely.

"It's Reese! That's Byron Reese!"

"Actually, it's not," Blackburn said. "There's no such person as Byron Reese. We looked up the info that Maggie gave us and it's all bogus --- but very well done. It could have fooled anyone."

"How about the bank account?" I asked. "Could you trace where the initial deposit originated?"

"It came from an offshore account in the Bahamas. Another dead end."

"So it was this 'Reese' guy who whacked Scarpelli?"

"Apparently it was."

"But how --- how could he have possibly gotten into Leavenworth?"

"He couldn't have --- at least not without a lot of help --- from someone high up on the food chain. A lot of people had to look the other way."

"That certainly could be explained by some of the names in that metal box."

"I presume you're referring to Senator Joshua Griffin, the chairman of the Senate Committee on the Judiciary, and Grant Langston, the Director of the Federal Bureau of Prisons?"

"Well, that certainly ought to be enough chops to get the job done."

"Indeed it would be, Walt, "Blackburn said, "but they're just names in a box. There's nothing there that specifically ties them to the Scarpelli thing."

"The same is true with the other names," Finch said. "They're certainly persons of interest in this case, but we have no hard evidence."

"With well-connected people like this," Greely said, "we can't just barge into their Federal offices and start slinging mud. We'd find ourselves assigned to some Alaskan outpost."

"I have a suggestion where you might start," I said. "Use your resources and find out how many of these high rollers have stock in major pharmaceutical companies. I'll bet you'll be surprised."

"In the interim," Blackburn said, "let's not mention the contents of the metal box to anyone outside this room."

When I arrived at home that afternoon, Maggie met me at the door.

"Walt, do you know what today is?"

"I don't know --- Tuesday?"

"No silly. The date."

I thought for a minute and then it dawned on me.

"Oh crap! We forgot! We've been so tied up with this Byron Reese thing we've forgotten Mary's birthday!"

Birthdays have different meaning to different people.

Maggie and I are a lot alike; most of the time, birthdays for us are just an occasion to go out and enjoy a good meal together. Every once in awhile there's a special one --- like our sixty-fifth --- sort of a milestone.

In the beginning of our relationship, we made the deal that we would avoid the hassle and pressure of buying each other the 'perfect' gift for birthdays and holidays. At our age, just being together was gift enough.

If on any given day, we saw something that we knew the other would enjoy, we would buy it, whether it was a holiday or not.

When our friends are racking their brains trying to find just the 'right' gift on the day before Christmas, Maggie and I are enjoying a nice dinner or a movie together.

Mary Murphy is another story altogether.

In her mind, I'm sure that her birthday should be a national holiday like George Washington or Martin Luther King.

To forget her birthday is a personal affront that would not be easily forgiven.

"What are we going to do?" I asked.

"The Professor saved the day," she replied. "He keeps track of those things. He and the rest of the gang have prepared a surprise party for her. Jerry and your dad have been out shopping and they've got everything ready to go."

"Jerry and my dad? --- planning a party? --- are you sure that's the best thing?"

"We don't really have a choice, now do we?"

"I suppose not. So how's this going to work?"

"Like I said, it's a surprise. Mary hasn't heard from anyone today, so she probably thinks everyone has forgotten. Your dad was just waiting until you got home. He's ordering stuff from Pizza Hut. Jerry got a cake from HyVee. We'll all show up at Mary's and surprise her."

*"What could possibly go wrong with that?"* I wondered.

The plans for the 'birthday bash' were set in motion and we all headed over to the Three Trails to surprise Mary, but when we arrived, the surprise was on us.

Mary wasn't there.

Old man Feeney was sitting on the porch.

"Mr. Feeney," I said, "Have you seen Mary?"

"I seen her take out o' here 'bout four o'clock."

"Did she say where she was going?"

"Didn' say nothing' to me 'cept "Get your ass out o' my way." But I heard her mumble somethin' 'bout "nobody gives a damn, so I'll just go treat myself to a movie."

*"Oh, boy!"* I thought. *"She's pissed!"*

Jerry looked at his watch. "It's almost six thirty. She should be along most anytime. Let's get ready and wait for her in the bushes. I made a run to Spencer's at the mall. Got some really cool stuff."

For Jerry, 'getting ready' was to put a big pile of plastic dog poop right in front of Mary's door.

I was dreading the evening already.

I can only imagine what we looked like, six old fogies hiding in the bushes staring at a pile of fake dog poop.

I heard Bernice say, "Shhhh! Here she comes."

We crouched low to the ground and watched her climb the steps.

When she reached her door, she looked down, "Well damn! Some dog went and crapped on my porch. Well, at least someone thought enough of me to leave me a gift on my birthday --- even if it was a dog."

We figured that was our cue, so we all jumped out of the bushes and yelled, "SURPRISE! HAPPY BIRTHDAY, MARY!"

Needless to say, Mary was startled.

"Jesus! You scared me so bad I think I peed my pants."

Then she looked at each of us. "You didn't forget! Thank you so much."

I knew that I'd forgotten and I felt about three inches tall.

Jerry picked up the plastic poop and we all piled into Mary's little apartment.

Finally the pizza guy arrived and we passed around the pizza, bread sticks and chicken wings.

We were all eating and drinking and having a generally good time when Mary let out a scream. "Oh my god! That's disgusting!"

We looked where she was pointing and saw a big brown cockroach in her glass of fruit punch.

Jerry couldn't help himself. He burst out laughing and pulled the old 'bug in a plastic ice cube' out of her drink.

"Ok buster," she said, grabbing Jerry by the collar. "First the dog poop and now the cockroach. I don't know how you're used to celebrating birthdays at your house, but one more incident like this and I'm gonna make a coin purse outta your nut sack! Got it!"

"Yes, ma'am," he said. "But what a waste of good plastic vomit."

I think most of us were relieved that Mary had cut him off before his grand finale.

The tide of conversation turned to favorite birthdays past and special presents that we had received.

When the Professor spoke, we all expected something philosophical and profound.

"Forget about the past; you can't change it.

"Forget about the future; you can't predict it.

"Forget about the present; I didn't get you one!"

No one spoke and the Professor grinned, "Fooled you. Didn't I?"

Then Jerry broke in. "Mary, you've been a really good friend to me. I apologize for all the goofy stuff tonight.

"I wanted to get you a special present for your birthday. I thought and thought because I wanted it to be perfect.

"Then it dawned on me. They say diamonds are a girl's best friend and you're my special girl, so I got you something with lots of diamonds."

Mary seemed touched until Jerry reached in his pocket and handed her a pack of playing cards.

Mary reached for Jerry's neck, but he was too quick for her.

I was stuffed to the gills as was most everyone, but Mary couldn't quit eating.

"I just love these buffalo wings," she said poking another one in her mouth.

She would suck the sauce off of it, then spit out the bones and gristle.

She gave a big suck and a funny look came over her face. She grabbed her throat and her face began to turn red.

She began flailing her hands and her eyes rolled back in her head.

I jumped up to help her but Jerry beat me to it.

He turned her sideways in her chair, bent her forward, put his hands around her waist, lifted her big boobs and gave her the best Heimlich maneuver that I had ever seen.

A big blob of chicken gristle landed on the table.

"Congratulations!" he said proudly. "You just gave birth to chicken little."

When Mary could finally talk, all she could say was, "You grabbed my boobs!"

"Mary," I said, "Jerry probably saved your life!"

"You just wanted to 'cop a feel' didn't you, you little pervert? Well I warned you."

Jerry was so stunned, he didn't move fast enough to get away this time.

She grabbed him around the neck and gave him the biggest hug in the world.

We all heaved a sigh of relief when she whispered in his ear, "Thank you."

I knew this was not going to be an ordinary birthday, and it certainly turned out to be one for the books.

# CHAPTER 20

The hawk-faced man's eyes were red and swollen from the insecticide that the old man had sprayed, but he knew that his eyes were the least of his problems.

He had to face Warren Westcott again --- empty-handed.

He heard the door open and steeled himself for the tirade he knew was coming.

But Westcott surprised him. He calmly took his seat behind the massive desk and just stared with a look that he hadn't seen before.

Westcott finally spoke. "So tell me, you're a professional assassin who came to us highly recommended. How does an old man get the best of a man of your reputation twice in a row?"

The hawk-faced man didn't answer immediately. He knew he must choose his words carefully.

"There were --- unforeseen circumstances --- things that were --- out of my control --- that I had no way of predicting."

"But isn't predicting and controlling circumstances and getting results what we're paying you for?"

"You ... it is ... I have no excuse."

"In spite of the fact that you failed to purchase the Ward Parkway house, we may not have been damaged. My sources tell me that all they found in the hidden room was more cocaine and other evidence tying Scarpelli to the Columbians."

"I'm relieved to hear that," the hawk-faced man said.

"But that still doesn't take care of our problem with Dr. Pearson and that damned study.

"I'm giving you one final chance to redeem yourself."

"I appreciate that."

"The cops have kept Pearson under wraps since your last bungled attempt. He's been nowhere except his home and his clinic which are both under heavy surveillance, thanks to you.

"This Friday evening, Dr. Pearson and his wife will be celebrating their anniversary at the Kauffman Center for the Performing Arts. The security will be tight, but I have arranged for you to be an usher at the theatre.

"This should allow you close access to the doctor's party. You can finish the job and disappear into the panic-stricken crowd."

"An excellent plan, sir."

"Don't fail me again. This will be your last chance."

"I understand."

When the hawk-faced man left, Westcott picked up the phone. "It's all set. The fool will be at the Kauffman Center Friday evening dressed as an usher.

"Contact Chavez and give him the details of the assignment. Once we eliminate this bungling idiot, there will be no one to tie us to any of the killings or that damned study."

# CHAPTER 21

After squad meeting on Thursday morning, the Captain asked Ox and I and four other officers to join him in his office.

One of the officers was Vince Spaulding.

In the past two and a half years, Vince and I have had the opportunity to work together on several cases and he has become a fine cop.

In one of these cases, Vince and I had gone undercover as a gay couple at the Cozy Corner bar; an assignment that still inspires wisecracks and good-natured ribbing from our fellow officers.

"Gentlemen," the Captain said. "You've all been working very hard on the Pearson surveillance team. That assignment is about to present a new challenge for us.

"Dr. Pearson and his wife, Katherine, have been pretty much confined to their home while this killer's been on the loose.

"Tomorrow is their anniversary and they have had long standing plans to attend the Kauffman Center for the Performing Arts.

"They're going to the theatre and it's our job to keep them safe."

"Surely the killer wouldn't try something in a crowded theatre," someone said.

"Are you forgetting where Abraham Lincoln met his death?" the Captain answered.

"Oh --- right!"

"You will escort the Pearsons from their home to the theatre.

"They are seated in a special box section called the Parterre. There are only sixteen seats in that section and we will have four of them.

"Ox and Walt will be seated with the Pearsons and the rest of you will either have seat assignments in adjoining boxes or will be stationed in the corridors on the Parterre level.

"They are never to be left alone. You will even accompany them to the rest room."

I looked around the room and raised my hand.

"Yes, Walt," the Captain said.

"Uhhh, which one of us is going in the ladies room with Mrs. Pearson?"

A strange look came over the Captain's face.

"Well, I suppose that's a detail we've overlooked. Thanks for bringing it to my attention. Do you suppose Maggie would be interested in going?"

"I think I can persuade her," I said, grinning.

"Very well, then," the Captain said. "Your assignments are posted. Let's all be safe."

I knew that Maggie would be thrilled.

The show was titled *'The Million Dollar Quartet'.*

On December 4th, 1956, four young singers in the infancy of their careers, came together in the Sun Records studio in Memphis, Tennessee, for a jam session.

Those budding super stars were Johnny Cash, Carl Perkins, Jerry Lee Lewis and Elvis Presley.

Well, the rest is history.

Maggie had been bugging me to see the show, but it just hadn't worked out.

Another plus was that this was saving us a pot full of money. The tickets weren't cheap.

On Friday evening, we gathered at the Pearson's house.

The Pearsons and Maggie rode with Ox and I. Motorcycle cops in the front and rear escorted us.

The casual observer might have mistaken our little convoy as a visit from a visiting dignitary.

We were dressed in plain clothes as were the other officers positioned throughout the theatre.

We parked and made our way through the crowded auditorium and waited in line for our turn to be escorted to our seats.

The ushers were dressed in funny little suits and caps that reminded me of the guy in the old Philip Morris cigarette commercials.

An usher approached us and suddenly veered away toward another line of patrons waiting across the room.

I was about to mention this to Ox when another usher approached and led us to our seats.

The lights went down and the curtain went up without incident.

The show was everything I had hoped for.

The young actors were, of course, not as great as the music legends they were portraying, but they did a decent job.

The music was fantastic.

Johnny Cash belted out *Ghost Riders In The Sky;* Carl Perkins sang his signature song, *Blue Suede Shoes;* Elvis swiveled his hips to *Hound Dog* and Jerry Lee Lewis thumped out *Whole Lotta Shakin' Going On,* just as the curtain dropped for intermission.

The crowd erupted in thunderous applause, the lights came up and patrons made a beeline to either the concession stand or the can.

Maggie tapped me on the shoulder. "Katherine and I are going to powder our noses. Any special instructions?"

I motioned to Vince who was standing by the door. "Take Vince with you. He will wait outside the ladies room and escort you back."

I asked Dr. Pearson if he needed to powder his nose, but he said that he was fine, so we just stood and stretched our legs.

After about ten minutes the lights dimmed, which was the signal for everyone to return to their seats for the second half of the show.

When the lights came up again, I noticed the usher that had veered away from us, standing at the top of the steps of our box.

Then I noticed something else.

He was pointing a gun at Dr. Pearson.

I yelled and crashed into Pearson just as the usher fired and I felt the impact of the bullet as it struck the back of the seat in front of us.

Almost simultaneously, I heard another shot and figured it was one of the officers returning fire.

I saw the usher grab his arm and look in the direction of the second shooter.

He looked at the doctor and me and then at the second shooter. He hesitated only briefly before firing a round at the second shooter.

I heard a scream and saw a man in the next section drop to the ground.

All this had occurred in just a matter of seconds and I saw the officers converging on the wounded usher.

He gave the doctor one last look and sprinted for the hallway.

I ran after him and reached the doorway just in time to see Vince on his knee with his revolver pointed at the advancing usher.

For a second time, I thought I was watching a Bruce Lee movie.

The usher leaped into the air and on his way down, one foot kicked the gun from Vince's hand and the other foot crashed into his chest, knocking him flat on his back.

This aerial acrobatic dislodged the cap from the usher's head and I recognized our old nemesis, Byron Reese.

By this time four officers were pointing their guns at the usher.

"Drop the gun and get down on the ground!" Ox bellowed.

Instead, Reese made a grab for the first person he could reach and pointed the gun to her head.

He had grabbed Maggie!

Slowly, he retreated toward an exit door with all of us following with guns drawn.

With the crowd behind him and with Maggie in his grasp no one could risk a shot.

Just as he reached the exit door, I heard Maggie shout, "You killed my buyers, you son-of-a-bitch."

I saw her lift her leg and ram the spike of her four-inch heels into Reese's instep.

He let out a wail and loosened his grip just enough for Maggie to forcefully plant her leg backward into Reese's crotch.

He groaned and Maggie slipped from his grasp.

Seeing an army of officers heading his way, he slipped through the entrance door and out into the night.

I grabbed Maggie and held her tight.

I figured she would melt into my arms, but the adrenaline was pumping through her so strong, it was all I could do to hold onto her and keep her from pursuing Reese.

When order had been restored, Dr. Pearson thanked us once again for saving his bacon.

He reminded us that if there was anything he could do for any of us, just ask.

He didn't realize at the time, just what that might involve.

My mind is filled with all kinds of worthless crap, and on the way home all I could think about was that stupid joke where someone asks, "Other than that, Mrs. Lincoln, did you enjoy the play?"

I was just thankful that wasn't something someone was asking Katherine Pearson.

# CHAPTER 22

The next morning after squad meeting, I met with the Captain and the FBI agents.

"You had quite a night," Blackburn said.

"That's an understatement," I replied.

"We may have to get that wife of yours a badge," Greely said. "I hear she's a pretty tough cookie."

"Don't encourage her --- please. One cop in the family is enough."

"So what do we know about last night's --- uhhh --- situation?" the Captain asked.

"The dead guy's name is Chavez," Finch said. "He's a contract killer. It looks like whoever hired this 'Reese' guy, hired Chavez to take him out."

"They were probably hoping Reese would take out the doctor and then Chavez would take out Reese," Barnes said. "It looks like they're tying up loose ends, eliminating anyone who could connect them to the clinical study killings."

"Any sign of Reese?" I asked.

"No," Blackburn said. "He's in the wind. After your wife nailed him in the cookies, he just vanished. He's a real ghost."

"What about the names in the metal box?" the Captain asked.

Blackburn just shook his head, "We're talking about some really powerful people; people who have connections right up to the White House. If we could have gotten our hands on Chavez or on this ninja guy, we might have been able to find out who hired them. But as it stands, we just don't have any evidence to tie any of these guys to the murders. We'll just keep looking for Reese and hope we get lucky."

*"Hope we get lucky,"* didn't cut it for me.

There was a cold-blooded killer out there who was responsible for at least six deaths that we knew of and he was still gunning for Dr. Pearson.

Passages from Kevin Trudeau's book kept running through my mind.

That evening, after supper, I returned to the book.

*"Companies, however, are run by people. People have two motivations - first, to make more money for themselves personally; and second, to increase their power, prestige, or influence. Therefore, the individuals who run companies will always make decisions based on what can personally enrich themselves."*

That certainly made sense to me. Greed, of course, was one of the seven deadly sins, and seemed to me to be the driving force behind most corporate decisions.

I read on.

*"I can tell you from first hand experience that the majority of officers and directors of major publicly traded corporations are greedy beyond belief and corrupt beyond belief. Making money and doing whatever it takes to make more money becomes their chief motivation in virtually all their decisions and actions. If making money means lying, stealing, defrauding, falsifying, or harming other people, it's OK."*

That certainly rang true for the names of the corporate executives in the metal box, but what about the politicians?

I read more.

*"The members of congress have passed a law which allows them to buy and sell stocks on, in effect, "insider information". --- The members of Congress have information that you and I do not have. --- Congress has passed a law allowing themselves to buy and sell based on this "insider information", and these stock transactions have been made perfectly legal! You need to know that politicians in Washington are making millions and millions and millions of dollars in profits buying stock based on "insider information"."*

Well, that could certainly account for the politicians that Scarpelli had mentioned.

I was sick to my stomach.

I'll admit it; I'm a Pollyanna.

I grew up with heroes like Roy Rogers, Gene Autry and Superman.

It wasn't hard to spot the bad guys; they all wore black hats.

Sure, there was evil in the world, but good always triumphed over evil.

I remember going to the movies and seeing the newsreels of our brave soldiers fighting for our freedom and for liberty and I was proud to be an American.

I believed that our government and the politicians we elected were there to protect our inalienable rights and freedoms.

Somehow, it seemed that someone had pulled a fast one on Lady Justice.

I just knew that I felt like crap and I needed to talk to someone.

I picked up the phone and called Pastor Bob.

"Hi, this is Walt Williams. I know it's late, but do you think you could spare a few minutes?"

"Hi Walt. Sure. We men of the cloth don't really expect to keep regular office hours. Come on over."

I'm not a church-goer, but if I was, it would be to Pastor Bob's Community Christian Church.

I met him several years ago at the real estate office. He had just broken away from one of the large main-line Protestant churches and was looking for a new place of worship. I found him an abandoned church on Linwood, not far from the Three Trails and he has built a fine congregation there.

I like him because he's not the 'stuffy clergy' type. He preaches not about dogma and doctrine but rather about love and compassion.

Like Doc Johnson, he's a cleric with a sense of humor.

I remember one day he said, "Sitting in a church doesn't make you a Christian any more that sitting in a garage makes you a car."

You have to love a guy who calls his bowling team 'The Holy Rollers'.

On more than one occasion, he has helped me through difficult times.

He met me at the vestibule door.

"So what's on your mind, Walt? Another moral crisis, I'm guessing?"

"If being disillusioned is a moral crisis, then yes."

Without going into the details of our case, I shared my misgivings about the powerful and greedy people who were running our large corporations and our government.

"I used to believe there were far more good people than bad," I said, "but now I'm not so sure. Is it man's nature to be bad?"

"Ahh, yes, the age-old dilemma; are we born evil or are we born pure and become corrupt."

"So what's the answer?"

"The answer is neither. We were born with a thing called 'free will'. Humans are neither inherently good nor evil, but the choices that they make in their lives certainly are. My job is to help people make the right choices."

"Seems like you have a lot working against you," I said. "There are a lot of powerful, greedy people out there."

"Indeed there are. The lust for power and wealth is difficult to overcome. It's an addiction. It's like the TV commercial for a brand of potato chips where they say, "I'll bet you can't eat just one!"

"You've probably heard the saying, 'money is the root of all evil', well, that's not true. The correct saying is, 'the love of money is the root of all evil.'

"Money becomes a problem when you put it above everything else. Money is there to be used and people are there to be loved. Problems arise when the opposite occurs; money is loved and people are used."

"I understand what you're saying, but I'm not sure it helps with my present situation. There are some very powerful people doing some very bad things and it all seems to be related to your 'love of money'."

"Then let me give you another thing to ponder.

"I'll paraphrase a scripture from the New Testament; "He who lives by the sword, dies by the sword."

"Consider that in connection with your current problem.

"You may find some enlightenment."

On the way home, I thought about Pastor Bob's words and suddenly, it was like one of those cartoons where the big light bulb comes on.

I knew what we had to do.

# CHAPTER 23

G reed is a powerful master.
I was convinced that it was the driving force behind the clinical study murders.

Powerful men, corporate executives in their ivory tower office suites and politicians in their congressional chambers had orchestrated this chain of events designed to protect billions in profits in the sale of pharmaceutical drugs.

And the FBI is telling me that these fat cats, by virtue of their positions of influence, are so well insulated and protected from the actual murders, that we can't touch them.

It was like one of those kid's puzzles with dots all over the page; you knew that if you connected all the right dots, a picture would emerge.

We just couldn't connect the dots.

Pastor Bob's scripture lesson kept running through my mind; "He who lives by the sword, dies by the sword."

If greed was indeed the motivating factor in their lives, maybe we could use that same greed to take them down.

After visiting with Pastor Bob, I was so wired I couldn't sleep, so I went back to my reading.

I remembered an article in one of the periodicals that Dr. Pearson had given me, *Alternatives* by Dr. David G. Williams.

The article was about cardiovascular disease caused by an imbalance of omega-3/omega-6 in the body.

This, of course, didn't mean squat to me.

The thing that got my attention was that it was determined that taking a fish oil supplement would correct this imbalance.

Fish oil was a natural product and available to anyone at most any health food store at a reasonable price.

Dr. Williams article read: *"our FDA has recently given approval to one company (Reliant Pharmaceuticals) to sell their particular fish oil product (Lovaza) as a prescription drug to lower triglycerides.--- Keep in mind that the FDA was careful about not approving or admitting that all quality fish oil supplements could successfully lower triglycerides, but only one product. By giving this one company's product prescription status, our employees at the FDA have not only given this company a license to steal, they have once again shown that they have absolutely no interest in supporting the public's health and well-being.*

*"Now if a doctor prescribes fish oil to a patient, the insurance company will pay only if it's for this particular product. The last time I checked, a month's supply of the fish oil 'drug', Lovaza, ran about $200 - compared to $20 or even less for an equivalent high-quality, non-prescription fish oil product.*

*"After this company received FDA approval to market the fish oil as a drug, in the first 9 months of 2007 (through September) they sold $206 million worth of the product."*

BINGO!

Dr. Williams had exposed the perfect example of collusion between the pharmaceutical industry and our government agencies, inspired by pure greed.

You gotta wonder how much of that $206 million went into pockets of corrupt FDA directors.

The tragedy was that they got away with it and are STILL getting away with it.

If only we could find a way to use that same greed ----.

Then it all came together.

I'll be the first to admit that my crime-fighting skills are more a product of *Turner Classic Movies* on cable than anything I ever learned at the police academy.

Let's face it, the academy lasted just a few weeks and I've been watching cop movies for decades.

My mind is full of cool stuff that Boston Blackie and Sergeant Joe Friday used to collar the bad guys.

One particular movie came to mind.

I rummaged around in the box of old VCR tapes that I keep in my closet and found it; *The Sting*, the 1973 classic with Paul Newman as Henry Gondorff and Robert Redford as Johnny Hooker.

I had just punched the tape in the VCR when Maggie stumbled into the room.

"Walt, are you aware that it's past midnight?"

"Can't sleep. You want to watch *The Sting* with me?"

She looked at me like I was stark raving mad. "You're kidding? Right?"

"It's Paul Newman," I said. "You know how you feel about Paul Newman."

"Walt, even Paul Newman couldn't get me to stay up until three in morning. What chance do you think you have?"

It's always good to know where you stand.

"Good night, Maggie."

"Good night, Walt."

I took notes during the movie and when it was over, I had formulated a plan to bring down the bad guys.

I had never pictured Lady Justice as a grifter, but she was about to launch a sting of her own!

The next morning, at my request, the Captain called the FBI guys for a conference.

When we were all assembled, I said, "Is it still your opinion that our chances of tying these killings to the names in the metal box are slim and none?"

The Fibbies looked at one another. "At this point, with the evidence we have," Blackburn said, "I think that would be an accurate statement."

"I have an idea," I said, "but before I tell you, what do you know about Al Capone?"

"Al Capone?" Greely said. "What's he got to do with this case?"

"Just answer the question."

"Ok, I'll bite." Finch said. "Capone was a Chicago mobster during the Prohibition years. He was involved in bribery, prostitution, murder, you name it."

"So was he ever convicted of any of those things?" I asked.

Finch thought for a moment. "No, actually they sent him to prison for income tax evasion."

"Exactly!" I said. "Now please keep that in mind while I explain my idea."

I had brought Dr. William's article, which I read to them in its entirety. Like me, they found it hard to believe that such blatantly illegal practices were occurring with impunity.

"It's a money thing," I said. "And they would do it again if the stakes were high enough."

"So what stakes are you talking about?" Barnes asked.

"This whole mess revolves around the clinical study that Dr. Mitchell conducted. If the results of that study become public, it will cost the pharmaceutical companies billions in sales and cause their stock to drop, hitting the politicians in their pocketbook.

"We'll use the clinical study as bait."

"Bait for what?" Blackburn asked.

"An exchange; tit for tat. We'll have Dr. Pearson find another natural product, like the fish oil in Dr. William's article and approach Putnam; you push through my natural product as a drug and we'll make the Rolotor study go away.

"It's a greed thing that they will understand. Dr. Pearson is tired of hiding from their hired killer and knows that his study may never see the light of day, so he concocts a scheme to get a natural product FDA approved and is willing to trash the Rolotor study in exchange for a percentage of the profits on the new drug.

"It's a win-win for both the doctor and Putnam. The government guys are in because they can use the insider information about the new drug to pad their stock portfolios."

Everyone sat silently, letting the idea sink in.

"It's a Capone thing," I said. "If we can't nail them for the murders, let's get them through their wallets."

Blackburn spoke first. "The only way this would work is to get wiretaps on all the names in that metal box. Do you have any idea how difficult it would be to get a court-ordered wiretap on a U.S. Senator?"

"I'll tell you where to start," I said. "Do some digging and find a Federal Judge who eats organic food and takes natural supplements. Show him what I've shown you and I'll bet anything you'll get your court order."

"You're not asking for much," he said.

"Hey," I replied, "I came up with the idea. You guys have to contribute something!"

"We may have another problem," the Captain said. "What makes you think Dr. Pearson will go along with this scheme?"

"A colleague of his has been murdered and he and his wife have been attacked twice," I said. "Leave him to me."

Dr. Pearson sat quietly while I explained my idea.

"It looks like you've been doing some homework," he said.

"I can only go so far," I said. "My understanding of all this natural supplement stuff is quite limited. This will only work if you can come up with a product that Putnam will believe is legitimate. Any ideas?"

"In fact, I do," he said.

He opened a notebook and pulled out another copy of Dr. David William's Alternatives.

"Read this," he said, pointing to a paragraph.

*"Antidepressants have become the most commonly prescribed drugs in the United States. Their use has doubled in just the last ten years. The latest estimate I've seen is that in 2005, almost 10 percent of Americans, or in excess of 27 million people, were already taking these drugs."*

"Antidepressants are as big a scam as the statin drugs. Let's face it. Everyone gets depressed. It's part of life. The answer, according to the drug companies, is to take their little pill. You can't watch an evening of TV without seeing a commercial for Cymbalta or one of the other antidepressants. The warning about the side effects take up half the commercial time, but the public just doesn't seem to care."

"Better living through chemistry," I said remembering Dad's pitch for Viagra.

"Anyway, Putnam Pharmaceuticals hasn't jumped on that bandwagon yet. I'm sure they're working on their own antidepressant, but they currently have nothing on the market."

"And you could give them one --- with natural ingredients?"

Pearson smiled. "Holistic physicians and naturopaths have been prescribing natural ingredients for depression for years. Depression isn't just about chemical imbalances in the body. It's also about stress, diet and other factors, but there are supplements that can help."

"Such as?"

"St. John's Wort, Omega-3's, folic acid to name a few."

"So could you mix up a batch of the stuff that would be convincing to Putnam?"

"Well, it not like baking a cake, but, yes, I think I could put together an all-inclusive supplement that would work.

"But we have another problem."

"What's that?"

"Research. Every big pharmaceutical company has a research and development division. In order to get a drug patented and approved by the FDA there has to be extensive research and testing.

"It's pretty much all a sham. The companies approved by the FDA to do the testing are publicly traded companies whose major stockholders are members of the FDA and Congress. But they have to at least go through the motions for appearances sake."

"What about the Rolotor study?" I asked. "That was a two year study. Would it be possible to use the subjects in that study, only substitute the antidepressant stuff for the cholesterol stuff?"

"But that would be illegal and immoral!" he said.

"Doc," I replied. "This whole scheme is illegal and immoral. That's the whole idea. If they buy into it, we've got them."

"You're devious, but clever," he said.

"So are you in?" I asked.

"If it will help nail these bastards, I'm in. What should I do first?"

"You have three things to do get this set up; use your alchemy to put together your magic pill; doctor up the test results to support your new drug; and watch this."

I handed him my copy of *The Sting*.

"I'm Paul Newman and you're Robert Redford.

"Let's get to work!"

# CHAPTER 24

The next morning, I was back in Captain Short's office with the Feds.

"He's in!" I said.

I explained that the doctor would be putting together an antidepressant made entirely of natural products and modify the Rolotor study to coincide with the new drug.

"Fantastic!" Blackburn said. "As soon as he's finished, we'll get the doctor together with Agent Barnes to work out the details of the sting."

"Whoa!" I said. "What's with the Agent Barnes thing?"

"He'll be working with the doctor when we're ready to put the plan into action," Blackburn said.

"Hold on just a cotton-picking minute," I said. "This con was my idea. I should be the one working with the doctor!"

"No offense, Walt," Blackburn said, "but we need an intimidating figure to go into the lion's den with Pearson. You don't exactly fill the bill."

"Right," Finch said. "The Wally Cox look isn't exactly intimidating."

"More like Barney Fife," Greely said.

I looked at the Captain. "Look, I've done all your dirty undercover work. I've been a 'john' in a strip club, half of a gay couple in the Cozy Corner Bar and I've even dressed as a tranny. You owe me this one!"

The Captain hesitated, "I can see your point, but I can also see what the agents are saying. Your stature doesn't exactly promote fear and trembling."

"I can be intimidating," I said. "I can do James Cagney --- or Edward G. Robinson -- is that intimidating enough for you?"

The Captain looked at Blackburn who just shrugged his shoulders.

"He's your guy, Captain. You know what he can do. You make the call."

I held my breath.

"Well, it was Walt's idea. I say we give him a chance."

"Swell," Blackburn said. "But he's gonna need a make-over."

"What kind of make-over?" I asked.

"Well, first, we have to get rid of the snow on the roof. You look like you belong in a nursing home.

"You're supposed to be a high-roller --- a savvy businessman sent to negotiate for Pearson, so you have to look the part. You'll need some new threads. I've seen what you wear and I'd have to say I've rousted guys out of the homeless shelter who dress better than you."

"No need to get personal," I said.

"We'll need to get you some creds," Finch added.

"Creds?"

"New credentials. You can't go in there as Walt Williams, mild-mannered cop. We have to build a background file for you because you can bet they're going to check you out."

"Right," I said. "I want my name to be Henry Gondorff."

"Where in the hell did you come up with that?" Blackburn asked.

"Just use it. I have my reasons."

"Then it's settled," the Captain said. "You guys get busy with Walt's new background and you, Mr. Williams, try to become as intimidating as possible."

That night, Maggie was ecstatic.

"Fantastic! Another girlfriend night!"

A year and a half ago, when I had to go undercover as a transvestite, Maggie got to dress me; wig, make-up, pantyhose, bra --- you get the picture.

Our first stop was the cosmetic aisle at the local grocery.

There must have been a hundred different products to choose from.

Maggie studied the selection and finally said, "Ahh, here we are; Miss Clairol's Gray Busters. What's your color preference?"

I examined my choices. "Might as well go all the way," I said. "Midnight black."

Other guys my age use Grecian formula or other such crap to hide their grays --- not me! To me, my hair is a badge of honor, of sorts. Kind of like the pin I received for being a realtor for thirty years. I figure if I've lived this long, I should flaunt it.

Besides, there are perks to being gray.

When Maggie and I go to the movies, I never have to ask for the senior's rate. They just take one look and give it to me.

We always shop for groceries on Wednesday because that's 'seniors day' and we get a five percent discount. Again, I don't even have to ask.

And speaking of free stuff, I've learned a little trick that drives Maggie up the wall.

When we go out to eat, especially if it's at a new restaurant where they don't know us, I pin on a big metal button that says "Happy Birthday".

I never say a word, but if we have a sharp server, more times than not, they will show up with a free dessert for the 'birthday boy'.

I don't do that at Mexican restaurants anymore. The last time I tried it, they put a big sloppy sombrero on my head, six Mexican guys sang 'Happy Birthday' in Spanish, and they put a glob of whipped cream on my nose.

The fried ice cream was good though.

We returned home and Maggie got me all lathered up.

"See you later," she said. "I'm gonna go read."

"Later? How long do I have to sit here?"

"The directions say 'thirty to forty-five minutes, depending on the amount of gray', so I'd say forty-five for sure."

"Swell."

Now I knew another good reason why I would have gray hair for the rest of my life.

Sitting there with nothing to do, I started thinking about the name for our new product.

It had to be something off-the-wall so it would look like all the other drugs on the market.

Who thinks up all these goofy drug names? Cialis, Prolia, Januvia, Zoloft, Luvox.

Maybe they hired Frank Zappa, the musician/ songwriter to name their products. He certainly had experience with goofy names. He had four children and he named them Moon Unit, Dweezil, Ahmet Emuukha Rodan and Diva Thin Muffin Pigeen. Go figure.

And diseases are just as bad. Who was the first guy to have a chest pain and say, "that feels like angina."

That thought, of course, reminded me of a joke Jerry laid on me one evening.

"A couple of seniors were about to jump in the sack for the first time. The old lady said, "Before we have sex, you should know that I have acute angina."

"Great!" the old man replied. "That'll make up for your saggy boobs."

I could tell that the fumes from the hair color were causing my mind to drift, so I tried to refocus on the name for our new drug.

Then it came to me. It was perfect.

I grabbed my cell phone and called Dr. Pearson.

"Doc, do you have a name for our new product yet?"

"No, but I'm just finishing with the alteration of the Rolotor study and that was next."

"Picadara! How does that sound?"

"Works for me. How did you come up with that?"

"It's Spanish for 'Sting'."

"Then Picadara it is!"

Maggie came into the room "Your forty-five minutes are up. Let's see what we've got."

Time sure flies when you're having fun.

Maggie rinsed the smelly crap out of my hair, dried it and I looked in the mirror.

My mane had been magically transformed from 'dirty snow' to 'midnight black' in a mere forty-five minutes.

"What style do you want?" she asked.

"You mean I have a choice?"

"Sure. Since you've changed your color, you might as well go for a new style."

I thought for a moment. "Cagney! Jimmy Cagney!"

Maggie got her scissors and comb, and in fifteen minutes my hair was parted in the middle and slicked back like an Italian goomba.

I spent the better part of a half hour in front of the mirror saying "Mmmmm, you dirty rat; you dirty rat!"

Maggie came in, put her arms around my waist and whispered, "This tough guy thing kinda turns me on."

I whirled, grabbed her by the chin and snarled in my best Cagney voice, "Look doll. Stay out of the bedroom if you can't take the heat."

I soon discovered that my little gun moll could not only take the heat, she could dish it out as well.

The next thing on my list was my wardrobe transformation.

The Feds had given me a 'company' credit card.

They said that since this was an official operation, Uncle Sam would foot the bill for my new duds.

Maggie and I went directly to Jack Henry, The Clothier For Men, on the Country Club Plaza.

I didn't know squat about clothes.

My last suit was from the Men's Warehouse. Actually, my last two suits because they had a 'buy one, get one free' special.

I went there because a guy with a beard on TV had assured me, "You're going to like the way you look. I guarantee it!"

How could you argue with that? After all, it was guaranteed.

Maggie told the guy what we were looking for and he brought out several suits for our approval.

I saw one I kinda liked and glanced at the price tag.

HOLY CRAP! That thing cost as much as my car!

"Remember, Uncle Sam is footing the bill," Maggie whispered.

Your tax dollars at work.

I said I'd take it and he led me to the fitting room.

I slipped on the trousers and the guy promptly shoved a tape measure into my crotch.

"Whoa, fella. We haven't even been out to dinner yet," I said.

His look told me he had heard that line before.

Maggie and I strolled the Plaza while the Jack Henry tailor was making the alterations.

When we returned, I slipped into my new suit.

My old suits just kind of hung off my shoulders, in spite of what the bearded guy on TV had promised.

Not this one.

It melted onto my body like a second skin.

Of course, at that moment, more of the useless crap that clutters my head came to mind.

I thought about the scene in the movie, *Hollywood Knights,* where Newbomb Turk says to an old lady, "Hey Lady! Did you hear about the guy with five penises? His pants fit like a glove!"

This suit certainly fit like a glove.

I left Jack Henry's with a new suit, shirt, tie and shoes that cost as much as a small condo.

When we arrived at the apartment, Willie was sitting on the front steps.

"Hey, Ms. Maggie," he said. "Who's yo' new friend?"

"Same old Walt," she replied. "Just a new exterior."

"Well som'bitch!" he said.

I knew I was ready. If I could fool Willie, I could fool anybody.

# CHAPTER 25

The hawk-faced man was hurting.

The bullet from the assassin's gun was just a flesh wound. It had passed through his arm, but it hurt like hell.

One of the cat scratches on his back had become infected and his instep was bruised and swollen where the bitch realtor rammed him with her spiked heel.

He needed a place to rest and heal, but with no money forthcoming from Westcott, he was forced to leave his comfortable suite above the Plaza and move into a sleeping room in a shabby hotel on Linwood.

Fortunately, the old woman who ran the place hadn't bothered to check for references.

After he had given her one of his most charming smiles and handed her two weeks rent in advance, she handed over the keys.

The move from a suite with a Jacuzzi tub overlooking the Plaza to sharing four pitiful bathrooms with nineteen other degenerate scumbags was, of course, a disappointment.

But he had been in worse.

This would give him time, away from prying eyes, to regain his strength and plan his revenge.

He understood why Westcott had sent the assassin. He had failed -- three times --- and he had become a liability.

He had no further interest in Dr. Pearson. That was Westcott's problem and he certainly wouldn't be getting paid.

He would still kill Westcott as well as his associates who had ordered his assassination.

It was just good business.

But he would also kill the old cop who had foiled his plans three times --- and his wife too.

This was personal.

# CHAPTER 26

On the way into the office, I was thinking about the movie, *The Sting*, and I couldn't get Marvin Hamlisch's snappy little version of *The Entertainer* out of my mind.

I was dressed in my new duds with my new hairdo and my new attitude and I was ready to kick some ass.

When I walked into the Captain's office, Blackburn rose from his chair.

I walked straight up to him, shoved him back in his seat and snarled, "Sit down, punk! I'm runnin' this show!"

Everyone sat in stunned silence.

"How's that for intimidating?" I said, grinning.

"I think that might work," the Captain said.

Blackburn smiled. "You never cease to amaze me, old man."

"Thanks. I'll take that as a compliment."

Dr. Pearson arrived and we were ready to begin.

In the movie, the story was divided into segments; The Mark, The Set-up, The Hook, The Wire, The Tale, The Shut-out and finally, The Sting.

I knew we wouldn't have all that stuff in our operation, but in my movie-buff mind, I wanted to play it as close to the script as possible.

## The Marks

The names in Scarpelli's metal box that were implicated in the Rolotor scandal read like a 'who's who' in political circles; Senator Joshua Griffin, Chairman of the Senate Committee on the Judiciary, Grant Langston, Director of the Federal Bureau of Prisons, Frank Brinkman, Director at the Food And Drug Administration, Harlan Glover, Chairman of the Board at Putnam Pharmaceuticals and Warren Westcott, Attorney-at-Law.

Blackburn had found a sympathetic Federal Judge who was not a stockholder in one of the major drug companies and had secured the warrants for the wiretaps.

With the wiretaps in place, we were ready to launch the next phase of the operation.

It was anyone's guess how many other well-connected movers and shakers would be implicated when the shit hit the fan.

## The Set-up

Scarpelli was an attorney at Warren Westcott's law firm, so we decided to start with Westcott, who was most likely the one who had hired 'Reese' to secure the clinical study, and work our way up the food chain from there.

Everyone was gathered in the Captain's office. Dr. Pearson had prepared the study for the new drug, Picadara, and the equipment was ready to record our phone conversations.

Blackburn looked around the room. "Everyone ready?"

Seeing nods all around, he turned to me. "Ok, Walt. You're on."

I dialed the number to Westcott's law firm.

"Law office. How may we help you?"

"I'd like to speak to Warren Westcott, please."

"I'm sorry, sir. Mr. Westcott isn't taking any calls."

"Oh, I think he will take my call. Tell him it's Dr. Pearson and mention the word 'Rolotor'."

"One moment, please."

"Warren Westcott here. Is this Dr. Pearson?"

"No, my name is Gondorff, Henry Gondorff. I represent Dr. Pearson."

"What do you want?"

"I believe Dr. Pearson has something in his possession you might be interested in."

"I don't know what you're talking about."

"Don't play games with me, Westcott. I'm not in the mood. You know damn well I'm talking about the Rolotor study.

"Now do you want to talk or would you rather read about it in the *Kansas City Star?*"

"Just hold on! What do you want?"

"Like I said, you want to get your hands on that clinical study and Dr. Pearson wants something in return."

"Like what?"

"First, call off your goon. If anything happens to Dr. Pearson or his wife, I've been instructed to go public with the study. Do you understand?"

Westcott hesitated. "Dr. Pearson won't be harmed. What else?"

"Dr. Pearson is prepared to surrender the study in exchange for something we believe you can arrange."

"Just what would that be?"

"Not on the phone, Westcott. I only negotiate in person."

Silence

"Tomorrow. Ten o'clock. My office."

He hung up.

I hung up and looked at my co-conspirators.

Smiles all around.

"You had me believing," Blackburn said, grinning. "Good job, Walt."

"Let's see how long it takes for Westcott to get on the horn," Greely said.

Almost instantly, a red light flashed on the computer screen. Blackburn punched a few buttons and we listened.

"Bureau of Prisons."

"Grant Langston, please. Tell him it's Warren Westcott and it's urgent."

"One moment, please."

"Langston here. What's up, Warren?"

"The guy you sent to take care of Dr. Pearson --- we've got to find him."

"I thought that was taken care of. Didn't your guy, Chavez, handle it?"

"Chavez is dead and your guy is in the wind. We have to find him. Pearson, or some guy named Gondorff, Henry Gondorff, who is representing Pearson just called.

"Pearson wants to deal. He's willing to trade the study for something — I don't know exactly what yet --- and he wants assurances that he won't be harmed."

"I don't know what to tell you. That guy is a ghost. That's why I sent him to you in the first place. He does his job and disappears."

"But he didn't do his job and that's why we're in this mess. If he kills Pearson now, this Gondorff guy will go public with the study. We've got to stop him."

"I'll put out some feelers, but don't hold your breath. And a word of caution --- you tried to have the guy iced --- he may actually be looking for you."

"Call me if you hear anything."

The line went dead.

"Woohoo!" Blackburn shouted, "We've got Westcott and Langston for conspiracy to commit murder."

High-fives all around.

"Before we all get too giddy," Dr. Pearson said, "It would appear that there is still a killer out there. It sounds like my wife and I are still in danger."

"Yes, you're right," the Captain said. "We'll maintain our surveillance. Hopefully this will all be over soon.

"Ten o'clock tomorrow, Walt. Are you ready?"

"I was born ready!"

# CHAPTER 27

### *The Hook*

At nine forty-five the next morning, Dr. Pearson and I pulled into the underground parking garage of the massive building that housed the offices of Warren Westcott, Attorney.

I had been fitted with a tiny microphone that would transmit our conversation to recording equipment in a van parked on Grand, a block away.

We took the elevator to the twelfth floor and stepped into the world of the rich and powerful.

I introduced us to a comely secretary who announced us to Westcott.

"Mr. Westcott will see you now. Please follow me."

Westcott rose from behind his desk when we entered.

He was a portly fellow, maybe ten years younger than me. He had fleshy jowls that wiggled when he turned his head.

He was dressed to kill and I noticed that he had given me the 'once-over' when we entered. I guess the FBI guys knew what they were doing.

"Have a seat," he said, motioning to two chairs across the desk from his. I noticed right away that our two chairs sat lower to the floor, requiring us to look up to see his face.

Strategic placement. Negotiating advantage.

He didn't offer to shake our hands.

"Henry Gondorff," I said. "This is Dr. Pearson."

"Mr. Gondorff, you said you represent Dr. Pearson. I've never had the pleasure. I thought I knew most of the attorneys hereabouts. With what firm are you associated?"

"I don't believe I ever said that I was an attorney. I said that I 'represent' Dr. Pearson. We're --- ahhh --- business partners.

"Dr. Pearson handles the technical stuff. I handle the 'business' end of things," I said patting the bulge under my coat. "Understand?"

"Uhhh, yes, I believe I do. You said you have a proposition."

"Sure, let's lay it all out on the table. Rolotor. It's all about Rolotor.

"That drug is important enough to you and your buddies to have Dr. Mitchell and his secretary killed to prevent his study from going public."

Westcott started to protest.

"Don't bother denying it. Let's don't get in a pissing contest here. We both know you hired a hit man. That's not what we're here to discuss."

"Then what?"

"You want that study to never see the light of day. We get that. Here's what we want in return; Dr. Pearson has developed a new antidepressant drug, Picadara, made of all natural ingredients.

"We want your buddies at Putnam Pharmaceuticals to push this thing through; get it approved by the FDA and get it on the market.

"All we're asking is a measly fifty percent of the profits."

I thought Westcott was going to have a coronary.

"The nerve! The unmitigated gall! Marching in here and making demands I couldn't possibly meet. I think we're through here."

"Calm down, fat boy. I'll say when we're through.

"Doc, how about giving the counselor here a peek into the findings of the Rolotor study?"

"I'd be happy to," Pearson said, opening his briefcase.

"Our study was conducted over two years. Three thousand patients with high cholesterol were given either Rolotor or our regimen of natural ingredients. Results showed that there was no significant difference in cholesterol levels; both were equally effective.

"Here's the kicker; the cost of the natural ingredients was ninety percent less than that of Rolotor, and there were no significant side effects with our regimen.

"Among the Rolotor group were nine fatal heart attacks, a significant increase in the incidence of diabetes, not to mention memory loss, inability to concentrate, impaired judgment, confusion, disorientation, irrational thinking, and other signs of dementia.

"Do you want me to go on?"

"No --- no --- that won't be necessary."

"So Westcott," I said, "if this gets out, Putnam loses billions in Rolotor sales and you and your buddies see the bottom drop out of your stock portfolio. Now let's talk about Picadara."

"But    I    that's not up to me."

"Of course it isn't. But I'm betting you know who can make it happen.

"Here's what we're gonna do," I said, handing Westcott a USB flash drive.

"This is our Picadara study. It's all there --- everything your buddies need to push this thing through. Let them take a look at it.

"Here's the bottom line; you guys play ball with us and Putnam gets a new drug, probably worth millions. They get to keep half, PLUS, they get to keep on raking in the dough from Rolotor. You and your buddies at the FDA, FTC and the Senate get to buy more stock just before Picadara hits the market and make a killing.

"It's win, win, win --- all the way around."

"I'll present your offer."

"Oh, and by the way, if they give you any guff, just mention the drug, Lovaza. They'll know what you're talking about."

"If we agree, you'll surrender all the information on Rolotor?"

"Oh, Counselor! Not a chance! We didn't just fall off the turnip truck. We didn't say we'd give it to you. We said that it would never see the light of day.

"No, that little study is our insurance policy that you big shots will hold up your end of the deal.

"As long as we have one another by the balls, neither of us will squeeze too hard."

"Let me see what I can do," he said.

"Here's the deal. The next time I call, I want you to tell me you have a contract prepared with Putnam giving Dr. Pearson fifty percent of the sales on Picadara. I'll pick up the contract and have our attorney look it over.

"If it's copasetic, we're partners. No contract and the world will know about Rolotor.

"Got it?"

"I understand."

Dr. Pearson and I walked the block to the van and tapped on the door.

Blackburn held the door open and motioned us inside.

"Absolutely fantastic! If I hadn't known that was old Walt Williams in there, I'd have bet on Cagney any day.

"And 'fat boy'! You called Warren Westcott 'fat boy' and got away with it. Really?"

Just then, the little red light started blinking.

"That didn't take long," Blackburn said. "Let's listen."

"Putnam Pharmaceuticals."

"This is attorney Warren Westcott. I want to speak to Harlan Glover --- immediately!"

"One moment please."

"Good morning, Warren. I hope you have some good news."

"Quite the contrary, Harlan. Pearson and his goon just left my office."

"GOON!" I mouthed in mock horror.

Everyone stifled a laugh.

"It's bad Harlan. I've heard the results of the Rolotor study. It would bury us."

"Yes, I was afraid of that. Our research is much the same but we've been able to keep it under wraps."

"What do they want?"

"It would appear that the good doctor is just as greedy as the rest of us. He has developed an antidepressant drug made entirely of natural ingredients that he wants you to push through the FDA and market. The bastard wants half the profits.

"In exchange, he says that the Rolotor study will disappear."

"Warren! You know we don't mess with natural products. There's just no profit there."

"They said you might say something like that. They told me to remind you about Lovaza."

"Right! The fish oil crap that Reliant Pharmaceuticals pushed through. It was a joke, but they made several million in profits.

"So if we railroad this new product of theirs --- what's it called?"

"Picadara."

"So if we market this Picadara, the Rolotor study will go away?"

"That's the deal."

"It could take months of testing to meet the FDA guidelines. Will they wait?"

"That may not be necessary. They have already tested the product. They gave me a flash drive with all their data. If it's solid, maybe our guys at the FDA test lab could use it."

"Email the data to me. I'll go over it with my R&D guys. If it holds up, we may have a way out of this thing.

"I'll be in touch."

The line went dead. The hook had been set.

# CHAPTER 28

### *The Sting*

It was now a game of 'wait and see'.

For the next two days, it was business as usual. With a killer still on the loose, we had to keep a close eye on the doctor and his wife.

We couldn't afford any mistakes at this point.

On the third day after our meeting with Westcott, the Captain called me into his office.

The FBI guys and Dr. Pearson were already there.

"Our friends from the Bureau have some phone conversations you'll want to hear," the Captain said.

Blackburn punched some buttons.

"This was recorded about an hour after you left Westcott's office."

"Putnam Pharmaceuticals, Research and Development Division."

"This is Harlan. Put me through to Mark."

"Yes, sir. One moment."

"Hi Harlan. What can I do for you?"

— footer —

"I'm sending over a study for a new antidepressant product. I want you to take a look at the data and see if it will pass muster with the FDA testing lab. It looks good to me, but your people are the experts."

"I wasn't aware we had anything like that in the pipeline. Where did it come from?"

"That's not important, Mark. Just take a look at the data and get back with me."

"There was nothing more until the next day," Blackburn said. "Then we got this."

"Harlan Glover."

"Good morning, Harlan. This is Mark."

"What do you think about the data?"

"Are you aware that this 'Picadara' is composed of all natural ingredients?"

"Of course I'm aware. What about the data?"

"I didn't think we ---."

"The data, Mark!"

"The study was very well done --- as good as anything we would have done here."

"So you could transpose the data to our R&D protocols and it would be ready to send to the FDA for testing?

"Yes, but ---."

"No buts, Mark. Just do it. Today! Get it to the FDA!"

"Yes sir."

We all just sat with our mouths hanging open.

"If you think that's juicy," Blackburn said, "just listen to this."

"Senator Griffin's Office. How may I help you?"

"This is Harlan Glover with Putnam Pharmaceuticals. I'd like to speak to the Senator."

"One moment, please."

"Good morning, Harlan. Good to hear from you. Have you taken care of our 'problem'?"

"No, Senator. In fact, there have been some complications."

"I thought that the operative sent to your man in Kansas City from Langston at the Bureau of Prisons was supposed to take care of things."

"That didn't work out well."

"So we still have to worry about that damned Rolotor study?"

"Possibly not. Dr. Pearson approached Westcott in Kansas City. He offered us a proposal."

"Go on."

"He has developed a new drug that he wants Putnam to market. He wants half the profits in exchange for dumping the Rolotor study."

"So the doctor's motives have not been exactly altruistic."

"So it would seem."

"Have you taken a look at the drug?"

"Yes, I just got off the phone with my man at R&D. He says the drug is viable and the data supporting it will pass the FDA tests."

"So what's the problem?"

"Time, Senator. I don't know how long we can keep Pearson waiting. The sooner we can get him on the hook with this new drug, the better."

"What do you need from me?"

"A call to Frank Brinkman at the FDA. If you can persuade him to push this thing through, we can put an end to this nightmare."

"I don't know, Harlan. I'd be stepping pretty far out on a limb."

"I realize that Senator, but consider the alternative. You invested heavily in Putnam stock just before Rolotor was released and made a killing. If Pearson's study is made public, we'll be forced to recall Rolotor and pull it off the market. Your stock values will plummet.

"On the other hand, you can dip into the till again just before we release the new drug."

"You do make a compelling argument. What would be Frank Brinkman's incentive to make this happen?"

"Brinkman has been inquiring about employment opportunities at Putnam for his son-in-law. It's possible that a very lucrative position in our marketing department has just opened."

"I'll make the call."

"Holy crap!" I said. "It looks like everyone's for sale!"

"We're not through yet," Blackburn said, pushing more buttons.

"Food and Drug Administration."

"This is Senator Griffin. Put me through to Frank Brinkman."

"Yes, Senator."

"Frank Brinkman."

"Frank. Joshua Griffin here. I need a favor."

"Always a pleasure to serve our esteemed Senator. How can I help?"

"I just spoke with Harlan Glover at Putnam Pharmaceuticals. He's sending a new drug your way. It would be very helpful if you could --- uhh --- expedite approval. He tells me that the data will meet all your specifications."

"Of course I'd love to help, but our approvals have been under close scrutiny."

"And for good reason, Brinkman. I seem to recall more than one instance where your administration has 'fudged' on granting approvals. A friend on the Senate Judiciary Committee could prove very helpful if those indiscretions should ever come to light.

"Oh, and I forgot to mention, give Glover a call. He said something about having a position open at Putnam for your son- in-law."

"Thank you, Senator. I'll take care of it."

"We've got 'em!" I shouted. "We've got'em all!"

"So it would seem," the Captain said. "Good work, everyone."

"We're not through yet," Blackburn said, pushing the buttons again.

"Putnam Pharmaceuticals."

"This is Senator Joshua Griffin. I'd like to speak to Harlan Glover."

"One moment, please."

"This is Harlan Glover."

"It's taken care of, Harlan. Now the ball is in your court again. Don't screw this up!"

I started to speak, but Blackburn raised his finger.

"Law office."

"Warren Westcott, please. This is Harlan Glover."

"Warren Westcott."

"Warren. Everything's all set. The study for the new drug is at the FDA and Senator Griffin assures me that approval will be expedited.

"Prepare our standard contract and have it ready for Dr. Pearson.

"With any luck, this will be all over soon."

"Consider it done," Westcott said.

Everyone looked at Blackburn.

"That contract is the last piece of the puzzle.

"All we have right now are these taped phone conversations. Once we have the contract in hand, we can move on these greedy bastards.

"Are you ready to make the call, Walt?"

"Let's do it."

"Law office."

"Warren Westcott, please. Tell him its Gondorff."

"Mr. Gondorff. I've been expecting your call."

"So here it is. Do we have a deal or is my next call to the *Star?*"

"Of course we have a deal. Like you said, it's a win, win, win situation."

"So let's get this done!"

"I'm preparing the contract. I'll have it ready by eleven tomorrow. May I expect you and the doctor at that time."

"We'll be there --- and no funny stuff --- you hear me!"

I hung up.

"No funny stuff? Where did you come up with that line?" Greely asked.

"It just seemed like something Cagney would have said."

"Well I have a question," Finch said. "Where did you come up with the name Henry Gondorff?"

"Yea, and Picadara? What's that all about?"

"Simple! Picadara is Spanish for 'sting' and Henry Gondorff was Paul Newman's character in the movie."

"I looked at Dr. Pearson. "You ready to wrap this up, Hooker?"

# CHAPTER 29

At precisely eleven o'clock, Dr. Pearson and I were escorted to Westcott's office.

"Good morning, gentlemen," he said, offering us a seat.

"So let's see the goods," I said.

"What? No friendly chit-chat?"

"We ain't here to chit-chat," I said. "This is business. You got the contracts or not?"

"Yes, I have them," he said, handing me a manila folder.

I took the folder and handed it to Pearson. "Here Doc. Look these over while I have a chat with the attorney. Make sure that fifty percent is loud and clear."

"So how much time are we looking at before this drug hits the streets?"

"Under normal circumstances, approval would take months --- maybe up to a year. But we have pulled some strings to get the process expedited.

"Once we have the signed contracts back in our hands, we can expect approval in about a week. After that, Putnam will have to gear up for production of the product. Then there's the advance advertising --- I'd say the drug will be available in a month --- a month and a half, tops."

I turned to Pearson. "Does that sound about right, Doc?"

"Yes, that's satisfactory. I'll take these contracts to my attorney. You'll be hearing from us soon."

Westcott laughed causing his jowls to quiver.

"What's so funny?" I asked.

"I was just thinking. Dr. Pearson set out to discredit Rolotor and now, it seems, we're going to be partners. Greed makes strange bedfellows, doesn't it Mr. Gondorff?"

"Yea, it's a real hoot!" I said, walking out the door.

The hawk-faced man was in the first floor lobby of Westcott's building waiting for the elevator.

When the door opened, he was surprised to see Dr. Pearson step out with another man.

He took a closer look and realized that the second man was the old cop who had given him grief.

His hair had been dyed and styled differently, but it was certainly him.

The old cop had nearly bumped into him and their eyes had met momentarily, but there was no sign of recognition on the cop's face, and for good reason.

He had spent hours transforming himself, applying prosthetics to round out his hawk-shaped nose, coloring his own hair and applying make-up.

His first impulse was to follow the cop, but he stopped.

The cop could wait.

Patience. Patience.

Today was for Westcott.

He stepped off the elevator into Westcott's suite of offices and approached the receptionist.

"Steve Douglas with the FDA," he said, handing her a card. "I'd like just a moment of Mr. Westcott's time. Tell him it's regarding one of his clients, Putnam Pharmaceuticals."

The receptionist spoke on the phone and then led 'Douglas' to Westcott's office.

"I don't believe I've had the pleasure," Westcott said, extending his hand. "I'm Warren Westcott."

'Douglas' turned to be certain that the office door was closed then went forward to take Westcott's hand.

"Oh, yes, we've met," he said. "But I don't think you're going to find my visit today pleasurable."

A look of recognition came across Westcott's face. "YOU!"

"Yes, it's me. Your man Chavez didn't quite get the job done."

Westcott was about to scream, but 'Douglas' put his hand across his mouth.

"We have some unfinished business," he said, "and I'm here to settle accounts."

He grabbed Westcott by the throat and as the life drained from the attorney's face he remembered the times he sat across the big desk from the fat bastard, swallowing his insults and wishing he could put his hands around his neck.

When Westcott's body went limp in his hands, he smiled. It felt as good as he hoped it would.

He propped Westcott's body in the big leather chair, took the phone off the hook and retreated to the lobby.

As he past the receptionist he said, "Mr. Westcott asked me to tell you that he'll be on the phone for awhile and doesn't want to be disturbed."

The elevator door opened and the hawk-faced man stepped inside.

# CHAPTER 30

The doctor and I hustled to the waiting van with contract in hand.

I handed Blackburn the manila envelope. "Is this it? Are we done?"

"This should do it," he replied, smiling. "We'll take the wiretap tapes and the contract to the Federal Judge. This should be more than enough to get indictments on all these creeps."

We started to leave when Blackburn stopped us.

"One more thing. The Rolotor study. Not everyone in the FDA is corrupt. I talked to a guy there we can trust. He said he would take the study and run with it --- that is, if that's what you want, Dr. Pearson."

"I'd be happy to turn it over to someone. That study has been nothing but a burden and it cost two of my friends their lives. It needs to be published so that my friends won't have died in vain. That drug is killing people and it needs to be exposed. I'll get it to your office today."

As I drove home I had one of those warm, satisfying, fuzzy feelings.

We had done a good job.

I thought about Kevin Trudeau's book. Everything he had said going on was true.

There was corruption, collusion, and payoffs involving corporate giants, politicians and government agencies, all geared toward duping the public and lining the pockets of the rich and powerful.

And we had the proof!

One thing that always bothered me was that Kevin's book had sold over two million copies, so the things he was writing about weren't exactly a secret.

So why, then, was there not a cry of protest from the public. Why no watchdog groups raising Cain? Why no congressional investigations?

The media was willing to jump all over some politico who couldn't keep his dick in his pants, but not a word on senators bribing directors of the FDA for the benefit of a large corporation.

It just didn't seem right.

It had been a busy and trying week.

I was exhausted and, even worse; my poor wife had taken a backseat to my involvement in the 'sting'.

But it was all over now and I was ready to relax, revel in our success, and give my lady the attention she deserved.

I put on my fancy new suit, compliments of the FBI, and we spent the evening enjoying a fine dinner and good conversation.

I slept soundly that night, believing that our lives were about to be back to normal.

I couldn't have been more wrong.

The next morning, the Captain called me into his office.

"Warren Westcott is dead! Strangled --- in his office. It must have happened right after you left."

I couldn't believe what I was hearing.

"His receptionist said that a man from the FDA calling himself Steve Douglas met with Westcott right after you left. I had Blackburn check with the FDA. They've never heard of a Steve Douglas.

"Did you see anyone as you left his office?"

"No, there was no one else in the reception area. No one got off the elevator when we were getting on."

Then I remembered the guy I had bumped, getting off the elevator. I remembered that there was something about his eyes --- dark, foreboding.

"Oh, crap!"

"What?"

"'Reese', or whatever the hell the guy's name is. I think maybe I saw him get on the elevator as we were getting off. If it was, he was wearing a disguise. But I know those were his eyes."

"Great! We've been looking for the guy since he murdered Dr. Mitchell with no luck. If it was him, we're no better off than we were.

"I thought this was about over, but if this guy's still in the city whacking people, then Dr. Pearson's still in danger --- and so are you and Maggie."

Days went by without incident.

I eagerly opened the newspaper every morning expecting to see headlines shouting, "GOVERNMENT OFFICIALS AND THE HEAD OF PUTNAM PHARMECEUTICALS INDICTED IN DRUG STING!"

But there was nothing.

My 'midnight black' hair had begun to grow out and the white roots were showing through. It looked like I was wearing a skunk pelt on my head.

This, of course, brought out the best in Dooley who insisted on calling me 'Stinky'.

Then, one morning as I was thumbing through the newspaper, I saw a small article on page four.

***"Frank Brinkman, longtime director at the Food And Drug Administration has announced that he is stepping down from public service and will be entering the private sector. Our sources tell us that he has taken a position on the Board of Directors of Reliant Pharmaceuticals."***

I couldn't believe what I was reading. I read it three times, but it came out the same every time.

I was about to fold the paper to take to the office when I noticed another article on the financial page.

*"Putnam, the pharmaceutical giant, has announced the recall of their popular drug, Rolotor. A spokesman from Putnam said that their studies had indicated that certain side effects of the drug needed further study before the drug could be re-released.*

*"Rolotor now joins other drugs removed from the market, Vioxx, Rezulin, Posicor and Raxar.*

*"News of the recall brought an immediate response from Wall Street where Putnam stock dropped dramatically.*

*"It was further announced that Harlan Glover, Chairman of the Board at Putnam was resigning his post."*

I was fuming!

Where were the indictments?

Where were photos of the creeps being led away in handcuffs with their shirts pulled over their heads?

Where was the FBI spokesman announcing the results of our 'sting'?

Where in the hell was Lady Justice?

I was so upset; I couldn't even talk to Maggie. I kissed her on the cheek, tucked the paper under my arm and headed to the station to raise some hell of my own.

I didn't even bother to knock. I barged in and found the Captain and Blackburn watching TV.

"I thought we might be seeing you this morning," the Captain said.

I was about to launch into my tirade, when he pointed to the TV.

"You'd better watch this."

The channel was tuned to CNN.

I was stunned to see the President of the United States shaking hands with Senator Joshua Griffin.

The announcer said,

"Again, today's top story is the resignation of Senator Joshua Griffin, Chairman of the Senate Judiciary Committee.

"This morning, the President went to Capitol Hill to personally thank the Senator for his twenty-seven years of service to our country.

"The Senator cited personal reasons and his desire to spend more time with his family as the motivating factor in his stepping down."

The Captain muted the TV and sat quietly as I tried to compose myself.

"Seven people are dead --- thousands of people are being poisoned by dangerous drugs --- millions of dollars are going into the pockets of corrupt politicians, and THIS is all we get!" I said throwing the paper on his desk.

"And what about him!" I said, pointing to the TV. "He's a crook!

"It's not that simple," Blackburn said.

"Oh really! Then maybe you can lay it out for me, because I sure don't get it."

"Senator Griffin was one of the President's biggest supporters in the last campaign. Without him, the President wouldn't be in the White House."

"BUT --- HE'S --- STILL --- A ---- CROOK!"

"Yes, he is, but he's also a kingmaker and kingmakers don't get thrown under the bus."

"Fine! What about Langston, Brinkman, Glover?"

"All under the Senator's umbrella. In one fell swoop you've probably erased the President's debt to Griffin."

"So glad I could be of service to my President."

"I'm sorry, Walt," the Captain said.

"Yea, me too," I replied as I walked out the door.

I was boiling inside.

I wanted to scream.

I wanted to beat the holy crap out of someone or something, but at my age and my physical stature, potential victims were few and far between.

I thought about old man Feeney at the Three Trails, but that didn't seem quite right.

I decided to settle for a run.

I went to my apartment and, thankfully, Maggie wasn't home. I really didn't feel like talking.

I put on my sweats and sneakers and drove to Penn Valley Park.

I took off down the path and I ran and I ran and I ran.

When I felt like I was going to drop, I ran some more.

On each lap, I could see the beautiful World War I Memorial rising majestically into the sky and I thought about all the countless thousands who had given their lives in battle to protect our freedom and liberty.

Then I thought about the cowards who were making a mockery of their sacrifice with their corruption and greed.

Finally, in the shadow of that great monument, I collapsed on the ground and wept uncontrollably.

I needed Lady Justice, but she just wasn't there.

I finally pulled myself together and headed home, but the euphoria that I had felt at the conclusion of our 'sting' had turned to depression.

I began to wonder why we even bothered to enforce the law when men of power and influence could walk away with impunity.

Maggie was home and I saw the look of concern on her face when she saw my sweat-soaked clothing and red, swollen eyes.

Without a word of question, she led me to my bathroom, helped me strip off the soggy clothes and turned on the shower.

I stood there, letting the hot spray beat upon my back until the water turned cold.

When I had dried and dressed, Maggie met me with a tall cold glass of Peach Arbor Mist, my favorite.

She led me to our loveseat recliner and sat beside me, holding my hand.

Finally, I said, "I guess you've sensed that this hasn't been a particularly good day?"

She just smiled and squeezed my hand.

In the next thirty minutes, I poured out my soul. I told her about the days events, my rage and my frustration.

She just sat quietly and listened without interruption.

When I had finished, she simply said, "I love you, Walt Williams."

It's amazing how one simple statement can make all the difference in the world.

I was about to pour my second glass of Arbor Mist when the phone rang. I was going to ignore it, but then I saw Mary's number pop up on the caller ID.

"Hi, Mary."

"Hi, Mr. Walt. We've got a problem over here."

"Of course you do. This seems to be the day for problems."

"What?"

"Nothing. What's up?"

"Some jerk brought an electric hot plate into his room and the damn thing blew a fuse. It's getting dark and we have no lights. I tried calling Willie on his cell. He picked up but said he was over at Emma's and this wasn't a good time.

"Any chance you could come over and replace the fuse. Oh, and don't forget to bring a flashlight."

*"Swell,"* I thought, *"I'm dead tired and depressed and I'm the one who has to go change a fuse while Willies over at Emma's getting laid. Perfect!"*

"I'll be right over."

Maggie had heard our conversation. "I'll go with you," she said. "You'll need someone to hold the flashlight."

We stepped out of the car and, sure enough, the Three Trails was shrouded in darkness.

In the glow of the streetlight, I could see Mary standing on the porch.

"Thanks for coming out," she said. "The guys were starting to grumble 'cause they couldn't watch their TV shows."

"Wouldn't want them to miss *Wheel of Fortune*," I muttered under my breath as I switched on my flashlight.

The hawk-faced man was looking out of the upstairs window when the car pulled up in front of the old hotel.

He couldn't believe his eyes when he saw the old cop and his bitch-realtor wife climb out of the car.

He had no idea why they would turn up at this fleabag dump, but one doesn't look a gift-horse in the mouth.

After squeezing the life out of Westcott, his next goal was to eliminate this couple that had thwarted his plans.

Tonight, they had been delivered into his hands. He could finish the job and vanish, as he had done so many times before.

He watched as the couple talked with the woman who had rented him the room.

Finally, she went inside, the old cop clicked on his flashlight and they disappeared around the side of the building.

Now was the time to act, before the lights came back on.

I dreaded the job that I was about to do.

The fuse box was located in the basement of the old building and the quickest way to get to it was through an outside stairway.

A hinged door made of corrugated tin covered the old stone stairway.

For some reason, this covered area separating the outside world from the damp and murky depths of the old basement, was the spot that every spider for blocks around, had chosen to make their home.

I hate spiders!

I opened the door and it fell back on its hinges.

I shined the light into the pit and its beam illuminated a thousand eyes staring back at me from silken webs.

"I really don't want to do this," I said.

"Maybe you won't have to," came a voice from behind us.

We turned and my light caught the glint of a gun being pointed at us by the hawk-faced man.

"We meet again, Mr. and Mrs. Williams. You've both been worthy adversaries. I respect that, so I'll make this as quick and painless as possible."

"But --- why?" I asked.

"Why, indeed! The two of you have cost me a quarter of a million dollars in fees, but more importantly, you have sullied my reputation.

"In my business, one is paid for results. I will take years to undo the damage you have done.

"It's just good business. I hope you understand."

I squeezed Maggie's hand as he leveled the pistol to my chest.

I was braced for the impact when a shadow from the streetlight fell across the gun.

The man saw it too, and turned --- but it was too late.

Mary swung the bat with all the force that her two hundred pounds could muster and the hawk-faced man's head split open like a ripe melon.

He fell to the ground.

I kicked the gun from his hand and felt for a pulse.

"He's dead," I said.

"Oh my Lord! What have I done?" Mary said, her knees buckling.

I grabbed her and held her close.

"You saved our lives, you wonderful old woman. That's what you've done."

# CHAPTER 31

The hawk-faced man was identified as Uri Hassan.

He had been trained as an operative of the Israli Mossad. He had turned rogue and become an assassin for hire.

He was linked to murders in Europe and the Middle East as well as in the United States.

With the death of Hassan, the odyssey that had been dubbed 'The Rolotor Sting' came to an end.

As I reflected on the events of the case, I felt compelled to go back to Kevin Trudeau's book for a second look.

His message was that there are more doctors, more hospitals and more drugs today than ever before, and yet, there is more disease and illness than ever before.

He attributed this to the fact that large corporations are poisoning our food with chemical additives, antibiotics and growth hormones, all in the name of 'profit', and they're getting away with it!

Pharmaceutical giants are pushing drugs with lethal side effects, all in the name of 'profits', and they're getting away with it!

Politicians and bureaucrats are lining their pockets with millions, using the influence of their offices to support and protect the pharmaceutical giants and food corporations, and they're getting away with it!

The English politician, historian and writer, Lord Acton, stated, "All power tends to corrupt and absolute power corrupts absolutely."

Everything I had seen in the Rolotor case supported his hypothesis.

All the players, from the Director of the FDA to the Senator, himself, walked away from this travesty of justice with a slap on the wrist.

WHY?

The answer could only be that our nation was suffering from a condition far worse than any of the drug-related illnesses --- apathy!

How could over two million Americans read of the atrocities in Trudeau's book and not be outraged?

Trudeau was outraged.

He wrote, *"That's why I'm mad as hell and I'm not going to take it anymore."*

Until the majority of the citizens of our great nation get 'mad as hell' this corruption is destined to continue.

Philosopher Will Durant wrote, *"A great civilization is not conquered from without until it has destroyed itself from within."*

The outcome of the Rolotor case was proof enough to me that a terrible infectious disease was rotting the very core of our great nation.

We pay homage to the brave men and women of our armed forces who give their lives in far away places so that our country will be safe from foreign invaders.

But who is fighting the battle against the forces that are destroying our freedoms from within?

My faith in Lady Justice took a blow with the outcome of this case.

Then, a strange thing happened; a notorious assassin who had eluded authorities on three continents, was taken down by a seventy-three year old woman with a white ash baseball bat.

Lady Justice taught me a lesson; one person, with a pure heart can make a difference.

# CHAPTER 32

A few days later, the captain called Ox and me into his office.

I was surprised to see Agent Blackburn with the FBI.

"Well if it isn't Henry Gondorff," he said with a smile. "Good to see you again."

"How may I be of service to the FBI today?" I asked.

Blackburn gave me a mischievous grin. "Is my aged David ready to take on another Goliath?"

I was still mad as hell that people of power and influence were somehow able to break the law with impunity and walk away scot-free.

"I might be," I replied. "What do you have in mind?"

"First of all," he said, "I want you to know that not everyone in government is corrupt."

"You could have fooled me," I replied. "Present company excepted, of course."

"Our little sting operation got the attention of some folks in the Department of Justice who are not beneficiaries of the pharmaceutical company's largesse.

"They had been concerned for some time about what they call 'selective enforcement' by some of our government agencies.

"The Rolotor drug fiasco that we exposed focused the spotlight on one of the worst offenders, the Food and Drug Administration."

"If your new operation has anything to do with weeding out the corruption in the FDA, then I'm in," I said. Then looking at the captain, "That is, if it's all right with Captain Short."

The captain smiled. "I think we can spare you and Ox for awhile for a good cause.

"So how can we help?" I asked.

"I'm sure you recall that the FDA has the authority to create a law, and one of their most absurd, states that only a drug can cure, prevent or treat a disease."

I remembered all right.

In Kevin Trudeau's book, *Natural Cures "They" Don't Want You To Know About"*, he gave an example of the absurdity of this 'law'.

He said that the disease of scurvy, which is a vitamin C deficiency, could be treated, prevented and cured by eating citrus fruit.

He went on to say that if a person were to hold up an orange and declare that it was a cure for scurvy, that orange would suddenly become a drug under their definition and the person making that claim could be arrested for selling a drug without a license.

His claim was that the FDA used this tactic, in collusion with the big drug companies, to keep natural products off the market, thereby giving the drug giants a monopoly with their expensive, patented drugs.

Blackburn brought me back to the present.

"One of the classic cases of 'selective enforcement' occurred in the late seventies.

"Through extensive research, a man and his wife developed a bread product, made of all-natural ingredients, that had the ability to curb hunger.

"Testing showed that it was effective in weight loss and that the natural fiber contained in the bread could potentially lower the risk of certain cancers.

"This, of course, drew the attention of the drug giants who set loose their minions in the FDA.

"It was a tragic case. The poor man did everything possible to comply with the FDA's requirements for a new food product, but they declared it to be a drug. It wasn't a drug. It was bread! But by their definition, he was selling a drug without a license.

"The guy fought tooth and nail, but in the end, the FDA had all the bread seized. There was enough bread to feed nearly a million people, but rather than give it away, they had it buried in a landfill. Bread!

"The fiasco included collusion beginning with the local FDA office, through congress and all the way to the White House. National television stations and major newspapers were involved as well.

"The man fought so hard that a friend of his who had inside information, told him that if he didn't back off, his family could be the target of an assassination attempt."

I could certainly believe that.

Our sting operation had linked at least seven deaths to the Rolotor drug cover-up.

"Truly a David versus Goliath story, for sure," I said. "So what is David going to have in his sling to take down the giants this time?"

"Elderberries," he replied.

"You've got to be kidding!"

"Nope," he replied. "Elderberries are our perfect weapons.

"Their medicinal properties have been known as far back as Hippocrates.

"They are high in vitamins A, B and C and they have a high concentration of a thing called anthocyanin, one of the most powerful antioxidants known to man.

"Among its other uses is the ability to lower the risk of cardiovascular disease by reducing the oxidation of LDL cholesterol in the blood --- and you know how up tight the drug companies get when you try to introduce a natural product that competes with their statin drugs."

"So how do Ox and I fit into this picture?"

"You're going to help us get the Bob Gordon Elderberry."

I had to think where I had heard that name, and then it came to me.

Bob Gordon and his wife, Kay, were the proprietors of Gordon's Orchard in Osceola, Mo.

Maggie and I had met them when we stopped at the orchard on the way to Branson.

Then a year or so later, another case involving religious extremists had taken me to Osceola during which time we made several more trips to the orchard for their succulent peaches and tomatoes.

"So what does Bob Gordon have to do with elderberries?" I asked.

"The University of Missouri Extension was collecting samples of elderberry germplasm to test. In 1999, Bob Gordon submitted cuttings of the berries growing wild on his land. After extensive research, his berry was selected by the University as the prototype they wanted, and they named it the 'Bob Gordon Elderberry'.

"I'm still not getting the connection," I said.

"It's the perfect setup!" Blackburn said. "Gordon has the elderberry named after him and he has a thriving market.

"We want to set him up with the equipment to process the berries into juice which he will sell in his market with a label that promotes the healing qualities of the juice.

"We'll run ads for the stuff that will get the attention of the drug companies.

"When they unleash their FDA dogs, we'll round up the whole bunch."

"So all I have to do is convince a seventy-year old couple to spit in the face of the federal government and the pharmaceutical giants?"

"Something like that. We'll have their back all the way."

"Yea, I'm sure that will be a comfort."

As Ox and I drove the two hours from Kansas City to Osceola, I tried my best to come up with a reasonable argument to persuade the Gordons to participate in Blackburn's hair-brained scheme --- but I came up empty.

How do you convince someone to put something they had built over thirty-five years on the line, especially when the outcome was unpredictable?

I had dug into the bread story that Blackburn had shared and I discovered that the FDA had completely ruined the guy and cost him tens of thousands in legal fees.

It wasn't exactly a persuasive argument.

We decided that the best approach was to just be honest, lay everything on the line and see what happened.

When we walked into the market, Bob was behind the counter wearing the same old leather hat I had seen three years ago.

"Hi Mr. Gordon," I said. "Do you remember me?"

"Sure," he said. You're that cop fella from Kansas City. You're too late for the peaches, but we've got lots of apples."

"Actually, we're not here just for the fruit. This is my partner, George Wilson. I wonder if we could have a few minutes with you and your wife?"

"Come on over to the house. I think Kay just took a pie out of the oven."

Bob invited us to sit around the big oak table in the kitchen while Kay was busy spooning big slabs of hot apple pie onto plates.

While we ate, I explained the reason for our visit.

Bob sat quietly until I was finished.

"I see a few problems here," he said. "First, I don't have the equipment to extract the juice from the elderberry and second, even if I did, I don't have enough berries to make the quantities you're talking about."

"The FBI has that all covered," Ox said. "They will install the berry presses and they have made arrangements for berries to be shipped in.

"The bottles are even ready with the labels."

"According to the story you told us about the man with the bread," Kay said, "the FDA could come in at any time and shut down the whole market and we could even be open to criminal charges."

"We hope that is exactly what will happen. We want the FDA to raid the market, but as far as any criminal charges, you will have complete immunity and the DOJ will reimburse you for any lost business."

"And for your co-operation," Ox added, "you can keep the juice presses and any profits from juice sales that come in before the raid."

"Plus," I said, "you get two extra laborers for free. Ox and I will be here to oversee the project to the end. The FBI is putting us up in a hotel in Clinton, so we will be just a half-hour away."

"I don't suppose we could get all that in writing?" Bob asked.

"Got it right here," I said, pulling a sheaf of documents out of my briefcase.

"You all have another piece of pie while Kay and I talk," he said.

I politely declined, but Ox gladly accepted another piece and dug in.

He had just put the last bite in his mouth when the Gordons returned.

"We've been at this for thirty-five years," he said. "We've been thinking of selling and letting some younger folks try their hand.

"Maybe this is the answer we've been looking for. If we're gonna go out, we might as well go out with a bang!"

It was settled.

A sixty-eight year old cop and two seventy-year old farmers were about to grab another pharmaceutical tiger by the tail.

The setup ran like clockwork.

The berry presses were installed, boxes of bottles with the incriminating labels arrived, and soon refrigerated trucks began unloading crates of elderberry heads.

While all this was going on, Ox and I were given a crash course in the orchard business.

We took turns in the field picking apples and Bob even let me drive the tractor.

I hadn't driven a tractor since I was a boy on my grandpa's farm. I was like a kid in a candy store.

But the thing that I wanted to do the most was drive the forklift. Since my high school days as a stock boy at the local supermarket, the powerful machines that lifted the huge pallets of groceries had fascinated me. The lift was, of course, off limits to a sixteen year-old kid.

At the orchard, the apples were brought in from the field in huge wooden crates weighing hundreds of pounds.

The forklift would carry the crates into an enormous walk-in cooler where they were stacked to the ceiling.

With some misgivings, Bob instructed me in the use of the lift.

The first time I tried it on my own, I saw Bob watching and his hands were behind his back. I'm guessing he had his fingers crossed.

Once the elderberry operation was underway, Ox and I learned to operate the press.

We discovered right away that another characteristic of the juice is that it stains --- horribly!

After my first day in the pressroom, I emerged looking more like Willie than Walt.

The bumblings of Ox and I that first day brought back memories of that I Love Lucy classic where Lucy and Ethel were in the big vat stomping grapes barefooted.

Thankfully, we weren't required to take off our shoes.

It wasn't long before the first bottles of elderberry elixir were ready to sell.

As promised, the Fibbies ran full-page ads in the Clinton, Springfield and Kansas City newspapers extolling the virtues of the juice as a way to control cholesterol levels naturally, with no damaging side effects at a fraction of the cost of statin drugs.

The day the newspapers hit the streets, the phones began to ring and cars began pouring into the market parking lot.

We sold out of our first batch in two days and worked late into the night to prepare more of the sought-after juice.

Sales skyrocketed, and for the moment, the Gordon's were pleased with their decision.

The bulk of the sales were for cash and Kay found herself making daily trips to the bank.

About ten days into the operation, Bob approached us waving a letter in his hand.

"I think you've got someone's attention," he said, handing us the letter.

The letter was exactly what we had anticipated.

## DEPARTMENT OF HEALTH EDUCATION AND WELFARE

*Mr. Robert Gordon*
*Osceola, Mo.*

*Dear Mr. Gordon,*
*Our investigation has revealed that you have been marketing Gordon's Elderberry Elixir with the label bearing a claim that your product will reduce the oxidation of LDL cholesterol in the blood thereby preventing cardiovascular disease.*

*Such claims and statements cause this elixir to be a new drug. A new drug cannot be marketed until the Food and Drug Administration has received and approved a New Drug Application (NDA) for the product.*

*In summary, it is the opinion of the Food and Drug Administration that Gordon's Elderberry*

*Elixir is a new drug and as labeled is seriously misbranded and, therefore, may not be marketed with its present labeling in the absence of an approved new Drug Application.*

*In view of the above and in the public interest, we request that you immediately discontinue marketing Gordon's Elderberry Elixir as labeled and immediately discontinue all distribution of promotional literature.*

*We request that you reply within ten (10) days after receipt of this letter, stating the action you will take to discontinue the marketing of this drug product. If such corrective action is not promptly undertaken, the Food and Drug Administration is prepared to initiate legal action to enforce the law.*

*The Federal Food, Drug and Cosmetic Act provides for seizure of illegal products and/or injunction against the manufacturer or distributor of illegal product, 21 U.S.C. 332 and 334.*

*Sincerely,*
*Reginald Baldwin*
*District Director*

Bingo!

This was what we had been waiting for.

"So what do we do now?" Bob asked. "Remember, I'm too old to go to jail!"

I assured him that nothing was going to happen, but if it did, we would try to arrange for he and Kay to have adjoining cells.

He didn't find that amusing.

I faxed the letter to Agent Blackburn and advised him to circle the wagons because the savages were just over the hill.

He liked my old west metaphor.

The ads continued to run and the customers continued pouring in.

We should have anticipated that the extra cash in the daily till would attract the attention of some unsavory individuals, but our attention was so fixed on the white-collar crooks, we weren't prepared for villains of the blue-collar variety.

One afternoon, just before closing, the gal that ran the register was filling the bank bag when a scruffy guy with a full beard and his hair pulled back in a pony-tail approached the counter.

Ox and I had just finished cleaning the elderberry press and were looking forward to a meal of country bar-b-que.

We rounded the corner just in time to see Mr. Ponytail level a gun at the clerk and point to the cash bag.

We ducked back before the guy saw us.

Our weapons were, of course, locked in our car.

Farm hands typically don't carry side arms, even in Osceola.

"We can't rush him," Ox said. "There's a good fifty feet of open space. He could get off two shots easily before we get to him."

Then I saw it.

"I've got an idea," I said. "You go out the back, circle around and wait for him just outside the door. I'll flush him out and you can take him down."

"So how will this flush thing work?" Ox asked.

I pointed to the forklift.

"An apple a day, keeps the scumbag at bay."

He nodded and took off.

I climbed into the forklift, fired it up and loaded one of the huge crates of apples.

I was hoping that the two wooden sides of the crate plus the four feet of apples would be of sufficient density to stop a slug.

I'd soon find out.

I rounded the corner, got my bearings and just as the thug raised his gun toward me, lifted the apples to block the trajectory of the bullets.

I heard the sound of the six shots and felt the impact as the slugs buried deep into my Honey Crisp armor.

The creep, being out of ammo and seeing the lift bearing down on him, turned and fled out the door, running headlong into a mountain of flesh.

It only took one swing of Ox's meaty fist to drop the jerk to his knees.

The sound of the shots drew Bob and Kay from their home.

Bob looked at the perp lying on the ground and then his attention focused on the crate dripping juice from the dozens of apples that had been perforated by the slugs.

His only comment was, "You city boys sure have a strange way of making cider."

It was business as usual for the next few days.

Then I received a call from Blackburn. He said that his informants had told him that the raid was imminent.

I hoped so.

I had been away from Maggie way too long.

She would drive down for an evening and we would have supper together, but it just wasn't the same.

I had just finished another undercover stint that had taken me away from home and now with this, I had been away from her for almost a month.

I had grown quite fond of Kay's apple pie, but it just couldn't take the place of Maggie's sweet kisses.

The day began like any other, the frost on the pumpkin melting away under the bright morning sun.

About ten o'clock someone pointed to Highway Thirteen.

Coming from the north was a line of cars that, at first glance, appeared to be a funeral procession.

A closer look revealed that the vehicles were big black SUV's and not stretch limos.

"This is it," I said. "Let's prepare a special welcome for our guests."

We knew that the purpose of the raid was to seize all of the bottles, juice and berries and put Gordon's Elixir out of business just as they had done with the bread company.

Bread was one thing, but sticky elderberry juice, the consistency of India ink was quite another.

We had figured out how to rig the storage vats holding the juice so that an unsuspecting interloper would have a rude surprise.

The SUV's rolled into the parking lot with red and blue lights flashing from under their grills.

They poured out of the cars with guns drawn and swarmed the market.

"U.S. Marshals! Everyone stay where you are and put your hands in the air!"

All of the market employees had known what was coming, but the half-dozen customers who had been milling about, stood frozen with fear.

The whole scene was reminiscent of the old movies depicting the Nazi Gestapo raiding a village looking for Jews in hiding.

Quickly, the guy in charge separated the employees from the customers.

He herded the employees into a corner and ordered us to stay put.

He grabbed a bottle of elderberry juice from the shaking hand of a terrified shopper and ushered the customers out the door.

When all that was left was market employees, he addressed the group.

"Which one of you is Robert Gordon?"

Bob raised his hand and stepped forward.

The marshal handed Bob an official-looking document.

"This is an order from the Food and Drug Administration authorizing us to seize everything associated with the production and sale of Gordon's Elderberry Elixir."

"Have at it," Bob said with a smile.

The marshals backed a truck up to the door of the market and began loading the bottles of juice from the display shelf.

When they had finished, they asked Bob for the bottles waiting to be filled.

He showed them where they were located in the storage area and the marshals loaded that too.

With that job completed, the guy in charge approached Bob again.

"Is there anything else on the premises associated with the illegal drug?"

"Well, if you're talking about my juice," he replied, "there's a whole vat of it back in the cooler that we were about to put in bottles."

The guy motioned for one of his underlings to check out the juice.

"What am I supposed to do with a vat of juice?" the underling asked.

"Our orders say to remove EVERYTHING associated with the drug, so figure it out!"

"Yes, Sir."

The man disappeared into the cooler and in just a few minutes we heard;

"OH SHIT!"

At that moment, another procession of SUV's stormed into the parking lot.

Blackburn hopped out of the car followed by small army of guys in FBI jackets.

"I'm Agent Blackburn with the FBI," he said, handing the marshal an official-looking paper.

"This is an order signed by the Attorney General ordering you to stand down. Please surrender your weapons and your car keys. We're taking you into custody."

The marshal handed Blackburn his weapon just as the underling emerged from the cooler covered from head-to-toe with black sticky goo.

Blackburn gave me a grin and said, "Well, Br'er Bear. Looks like we got us a tar baby."

We wrapped up the elderberry caper and headed home.

The Gordon's got to keep the berry press as promised and the Feds even gave them new bottles with labels more in tune with the current law.

Plus, he had raked in a bundle from the sale of the new juice.

The word spread rapidly that the Bob and Kay were part of an FBI undercover operation and they soon became local heroes.

On the day we parted company, Kay gave Ox a pie fresh out of the oven and Bob handed me a peck of apples.

"Got you some without bullet holes," he said, smiling.

Blackburn kept me informed about the progress of our sting.

The marshals, it turned out, were simply unsuspecting pawns in the 'selective enforcement' scheme.

Their orders had come from the Kansas City office of the FDA.

The order had been passed down to them directly from the FDA's Center for Drug Evaluation and Research.

The Center's director, coincidently, had a son on the board of directors of Martin Pharmaceuticals.

One of their most profitable drugs just happened to be a statin whose purpose was to regulate cholesterol.

Based on our work, the Attorney General launched an investigation into the regulatory practices of the FDA and its relationship with the large drug companies.

While our little victory couldn't be classified as a knockout punch, it was a start.

Undoubtedly there would be stonewalling and arm twisting, and congressmen and bureaucrats who had been on the take would be getting calls from the CEO's of the drug giants calling in their favors.

Years could pass before there would be any real reform in the system that had become so badly corrupted, but if it happened in my lifetime, I would be proud to say that I had a small part in it.

I had been in Osceola for the better part of two weeks and on my return, my friends and family insisted on throwing a party.

I appreciated the gesture, but my goal was some alone time with Maggie.

I enjoyed the laughing and the jokes and the food, but I was relieved when the last guest departed.

Maggie smiled and gave me her 'come hither' look.

I didn't have to be asked twice.

We had some 'catching up' to do.

I just didn't realize that we were going to do all our 'catching up' in one night!

A cop's schedule can be frustrating, but a realtor's can be just as bad.

A good agent must work when their clients are available.

Maggie had been working with a gal whose husband was being transferred into Kansas City.

They had pre-selected several homes in anticipation of his arrival.

His plane had landed and he was anxious to see the homes that evening.

Maggie called and said that she would just grab a quick bite on the run and that I was on my own for supper.

While I would miss my sweetie, I realized that this wasn't all together a terrible thing.

Maggie had succeeded in steering my diet from fried things to grilled things and from tasty starches to green things.

I was slowly being morphed from a carnivore to a herbivore, but old habits die slowly.

I figured that this was my night to pay Mel a visit.

Prior to my nuptials, Mel's Diner was my eatery of choice.

Most everything on his menu was either deep-fried or fried on the grill in butter.

I decided on a chicken-fried steak with fluffy potatoes, all smothered in greasy gravy. Of course it came with a huge slice of Texas toast, buttered and grilled.

I topped it all off with a generous slice of lemon pie with meringue three inches high.

I figured that I would have to graze on greens for a month to make up for my debauchery.

I left the diner so full I could barely waddle.

I was on the way to my car when two men came up beside me.

I felt something being pressed into my side and guessed that it wasn't the guy's finger.

"Just keep walking," the guy said. "We're going to that black van just ahead."

When we reached the van, one guy opened the cargo door while the other one patted me down.

I had left my gun in my car before going into Mel's. I suppose it was just as well. They'd have just taken it anyway.

After determining that I was unarmed, he gave me a shove. "Get in."

One guy hopped into the driver's seat and the other sat on a bench opposite me with a gun trained at my chest.

"Who are you guys?" I asked.

"I guess it really doesn't matter if I tell you since you won't be in a position to tell anyone else."

That wasn't a message that I wanted to hear.

"Apparently you've pissed off some very powerful people," he said. "The marks that my partner and I usually get are drug lords, crime bosses or other assassins. We've never been hired to do an old cop.

"They don't give us details, but I hear you've been stepping on the toes of some drug company bigwigs with political connections.

"That'll get you killed, you know."

"Can we talk about this?" I asked.

He looked at his watch. "You can talk all you want for the next ten minutes, cause after that, you won't be talking no more."

I realized that bargaining with a hired assassin was a waste of what little breath I had left.

I burped and got a second taste of the lemon pie.

*"Well,"* I thought, *"at least my last meal was a dandy."*

"Exactly how do you plan to do this?" I asked.

Then I remembered the old guy on the front porch of the Three Trails who said that if he knew where he was going to die, he simply wouldn't go there.

I didn't think that was going to be an option under these circumstances.

"We're professionals," he said. "No guns or knives --- too messy and they leave too many clues. You're going to have a terrible accident."

I looked out the window and saw that we were in downtown Kansas City.

The van turned into a parking garage and began to slowly wind up the ramps to the top floor.

I counted six levels before we reached the roof.

The driver parked and opened the cargo door.

"Out!" he barked.

They each grabbed an arm and drug me to the roof railing.

I looked over the edge. It was a long, long way down and I was afraid of heights to begin with.

I had heard of cruel twists of fate where guys who were afraid of water drowned and here I was, an acrophobic who was about to be tossed over the edge.

"Any last words?" the guy asked.

I turned to speak, but instead of words coming out of my mouth, it was Mel's delicious dinner.

Lemon pie, Texas toast, chicken fried steak and fluffy potatoes all smothered in gravy erupted and covered the guy from head to toe.

"Arrrrrrrrghhhhh," he shouted.

The next thing I knew, I was being hoisted over the guardrail.

I hung suspended for just a moment and a final shove pushed me over the edge.

The last thing I heard was the guy screaming, "Have a nice trip, you puke!"

I had experienced dreams where I was flying. It had been exhilarating. I would launch out and glide over the hills and trees and I always awoke refreshed and comfortable in my bed.

This was nothing like that at all.

I saw the pavement coming at me from six stories below and realized that I wouldn't be waking up in my comfortable bed.

About midway into my swan dive, I saw the red and white umbrella of a tamale cart moving my direction.

At the last moment I realized that the cart and I were on a collision course.

I suddenly realized the irony of the situation. I was going to die on top of a tamale cart and I didn't even like tamales.

# CHAPTER 33

When I opened my eyes, I was totally disoriented.

I looked down and there, far below, I saw the body of Walter Williams lying in a hospital bed.

The face was covered with an oxygen mask, bags of liquid were dripping into tubes inserted into the arms and an overhead machine displayed digital readouts of his vital signs.

Maggie was at the bedside holding his hand.

A small circle of friends and family stood quietly in the corner.

The drama being played out below, reminded me of a play in which I acted in high school.

It was called *Balcony Scene*.

I played St. Peter and my best friend, Kenny, played the part of a man who had died.

St. Peter and the man were in the balcony of the funeral home looking down on the service below.

The gist of the story was that St. Peter was giving the man the opportunity to see and hear what his friends and family thought of him, based on the life that he had lived.

Fifty years had passed and I still remembered the two opening lines of the play.

*"Are you sure we won't be seen?"*

*"Yes, I am quite sure."*

My first thought was that surely they must know that I am up here --- wherever 'here' might be.

Then I remembered that in the play, the guy was dead, and my second thought was wondering whether I might have cashed in my chips as well.

At that moment, a man in a white coat entered the room. The stethoscope around his neck led me to believe that he was a doctor.

He read the chart attached to the foot of the bed and then studied the digital readouts.

He spoke and I heard every word as clearly as if he were standing right beside me.

"The good news is that his vitals are stable."

"And the bad news?" Maggie asked.

"He is still in a deep coma. With a head injury like he sustained, there is no way of knowing how soon --- or even if, he will wake up."

He turned to the little knot of family and friends.

"You all might as well go on home and get some rest. He might regain consciousness in a matter of hours, or it could be days, or maybe never. He's stable for now and we'll call you if there's any change."

Dad came over and put his hand on Maggie's shoulder.

"Come on, honey. You need to get some sleep."

"I can't leave him," she replied. "You all go. I'll let you know if anything changes."

Each one, in turn, gave Maggie a hug, and a pat on the hand to the body in the bed.

After they were gone, Maggie laid her head on the side of the bed, never letting go of the limp hand.

I suddenly became aware of the presence of a bright light that grew in intensity.

I turned toward the light and saw a figure approaching out of its brilliance.

At first, I couldn't distinguish the features of the apparition, but when it spoke, I recognized the voice.

"She's quite a gal, isn't she Walter?"

Then, the voice and the figure blended into one.

"Mom! Is that you?"

"Yes, Walter. It's your mother."

I moved forward to embrace her, but she held up her hand.

"Sorry, son, but at this time, think of our meeting like when you were undercover as a 'john' at the Red Garter --- looky but no touchy."

"You know about that?"

"Of course I know. You're my son."

"So you're coming to me from --- where --- heaven?"

"Sure, let's call it that."

I had read about people who had died and were met by loved ones who led them into the light.

"So are you here to get me? Am I dying?"

"My goodness no. It's not your time yet."

"So what's it like --- up there --- over there --- I'm not quite sure of the terminology."

"I know it's confusing. Just try to think of it as an altered state of consciousness."

"Yea, that certainly clears everything up. But what's it like?"

"Unfortunately, this is a lot like the CIA. I could tell you, but then I'd have to kill you --- just kidding!"

I didn't remember Mom having such a warped sense of humor. Maybe that's where I got it.

"So what happened to me?"

"You don't remember being pitched off the roof of the parking garage by a couple of goons?"

"Of course I do. I was falling and --- and then there was that damn tamale cart."

"First of all, please watch your language," she said, looking over her shoulder. "Someone might be listening."

"So there really is a Big Guy?"

"Let's just say that there's an awful lot of stuff going on up here and somebody has to organize it."

"So if there's a heaven, is there a hell as well?"

"Oh, there's definitely a hell. I had to sit through a Taylor Swift concert the other night."

I guessed that hell was different things to different people.

"So let's get back to what happened to me."

"Oh, right. The tamale cart! You have no idea how much trouble it was to get that cart under you at exactly the right moment. The tamale vendor was ogling some chick and we had to employ some desperate measures."

"We? You said 'we'?"

"Sure, your grandfather and me."

"Grandpa is involved in all this stuff too?"

"Well sure. I used to be able to handle most everything, but since you got that wild hair to become a cop, I needed some extra help."

"Where is Grandpa? Can I see him?"

"No, not this time, but someday for sure."

"So you needed extra help --- doing what exactly?"

"Keeping your scrawny butt out of a sling. You keep getting in all those scrapes. Somebody has to pull your fat out of the fire."

I tried to ignore her mixed metaphors.

"What scrapes are you talking about?"

"Well, just the other day, you were about to be flash frozen in the morgue and as I recall, your last act was to send a cell phone message to Ox. Do you have any idea what your grandpa and I had to go through to get you enough bars to get that signal out of that freezer in the basement of that building?"

"You can actually do that?"

"And that's not all. Let's talk about your honeymoon in Hawaii. You just had to scale down a vertical cliff in a volcanic crater. What were you thinking? We worked overtime that day.

"And don't forget the lizards. Do you know how difficult it is to train lizards?"

"So you do animals too?"

"Of course. Cats are the worst and, naturally, you had to use a cat to take out the hawk-faced man at Dr. Pearson's house. Have you ever tried herding cats?"

"So it wasn't just a coincidence that I stepped on that cat's tail at just the right moment?"

She smiled. "Son, there's really no such thing as a coincidence."

"So, are you and Grandpa --- like --- angels?"

"Sure, let's call it that."

I wished that she would stop using that phrase.

"We brought you into this world. Just because we croak doesn't mean that our job is over. I'll be your mom forever, no matter how old you are."

It was actually a very comforting thought.

"Oh, when you get back, tell your dad that I said 'hello', and give my best to Bernice."

"You know about Dad and Bernice?"

"Of course I know. Not much gets by us up here."

"And you're OK with it?"

"We look at things from a different perspective. Your dad may have been a crappy husband and father, but he has a good heart.

"I know now that he loved us both and that's what matters."

"So you've forgiven him?"

"That's what we do.

"Oh, and one more thing. Tell Willie that his grandparents are really proud of the exhibit that he donated to the St. Clair County Museum. His family was a big part of the history of that area and now their story will be available for generations to come."

I knew that would please my little friend.

He had never known his grandparents even existed and now to be told that they were proud of him would mean the world to him.

We noticed some movement below. Maggie got up, stretched and sat back down beside the bed.

"You got yourself a good one there, son. What took you so long to pop the question?"

"I guess I just wanted to be sure we were doing the right thing."

"Well, based on what I've seen, you two are doing everything just right."

"Everything? What do you mean by everything? You see EVERYTHING?"

"Well we could. We're interested and we're concerned, but we're not voyeurs."

"Gee, that's a comfort."

Just then, there was a fluxuation in the bright light behind her.

"That's my cue," she said. "Like when they dim the lights at a play just before the curtain goes up. My time is about up."

"So what happens now?" I asked.

"Now it's time to return to your world; time to get back to Maggie."

"You never did tell me what happened when I hit the tamale cart."

"Well, thanks to my perfect timing, you bounced off that umbrella like it was a trampoline. Unfortunately, your dismount wasn't that great.

"You have a couple of cracked ribs, some bruises and you whacked your head on the sidewalk."

I felt my head and ribs.

"How come I don't hurt?"

"Because right now, your spirit is free from the limitations of your earthly body. Trust me, when you go back you're going to hurt.

"Oh, I almost forgot. You've got a job to do."

"Already? I'm still in a coma."

"Not for long. Don't you want to get those two goons who tossed you off the roof?"

"I think I got one of them pretty good already. I seem to recall hurling on him just before he hurled me."

"Yes, that was a nice touch," she said, smiling.

"So what's the job?"

"The goons aren't finished yet. You and Agent Backburn were both thorns in the side of the drug giants. They think they've taken care of you and now they're gunning for Blackburn."

"So what do I do?"

"Just keep your eyes open. You'll know."

The bright light fluxed again.

"Time to go," she said.

"Will I see you again?"

"When the time is right."

"I love you, Mom, and I miss you."

"I love you too, Walt. Always will."

Then she turned and disappeared into the light.

# CHAPTER 34

When I opened my eyes again, I was lying in the hospital bed and I was pretty certain that my spirit had reunited with my body, because I hurt like hell.

The memory of my out-of-body experience was still fresh in my mind and the warm feeling that I had from seeing and talking to my mother made the pain more bearable.

I looked around the room for Maggie, but she was not there.

Then I heard the toilet flush and saw her coming toward me.

I tried to speak, but the oxygen mask covering my face muffled the sound.

She sat down beside the bed and when she held my hand, I gave it my best squeeze.

Her eyes met mine and I gave her a wink.

She burst into tears and laid her head on my chest.

"Oh Walt. I thought I'd lost you."

"Mwwuummph," was all I could say from behind the mask.

Maggie pulled the cord attached to the bed and a burly nurse strode into the room.

My first thought was, *"Why do all my nurses have to look like Nurse Ratchett?"*

"So our boy's awake," she said, flashing a penlight in my eyes.

"How many fingers?" she asked, holding up two.

"Murrromph," I replied.

She lifted the mask off my face.

"Two!"

"How do you feel?"

"Like I just fell six stories from a parking garage. Other than that, fine."

"Sense of humor. Good sign," she said.

She was about to re-mask me.

"Can you please leave that off? I can breathe just fine --- well maybe except for the pain in my ribs."

She checked the monitors.

"Sure."

Having regained full consciousness, I became aware of a strange sensation in my private parts.

I looked at Maggie. "Mr. Winky! He didn't get crushed, did he?"

"No silly. You have a catheter."

I had heard of those things before and they terrified me.

"How --- who hooked me up?"

Nurse Ratchett smiled a knowing smile. "That would be me."

*"Swell,"* I thought. *"There's no such thing as dignity in a hospital."*

After she had finished probing and poking, the nurse left the room.

"How long have I been here?" I asked.

"This is the second day. I'm so relieved. The doctor wasn't sure that you'd wake up at all."

"You can't get rid of me that easy."

Seeing that I was back among the living, Maggie pulled out her phone.

"I promised everyone that I would call as soon as you woke up. I'm going to make those calls. You just rest."

She made the calls and that initiated a flood of visitors.

Friends, family, cops and even old realtor friends stopped by to wish me well.

Each one, of course, had to bring a flower or a balloon of some sort and before long, my room looked like kid's day at Chuckie Cheese.

The captain was one of my first visitors.

He brought a stenographer to take my statement about the abduction and attempted murder.

When I told him what the thug had said about pissing off some very powerful people in the drug industry, he was furious.

"We have to catch those guys and find out who hired them. Unless we can tie these assassins to one of the executives, they'll just keep coming after our people."

He had mug books delivered to the hospital and I spent hours looking at photos of scumbags, but they just weren't there.

On a lighter note, he pointed out that this was the third tamale cart that the City had to buy for Jim's Famous Tamales.

In addition to the one I had just squashed, another had been blow up during the Gay Pride Parade and I had t-boned a third one while driving a bomb in a trolley car to Loose Park Lake.

On one occasion, Dad had stopped by.

It was just the two of us.

I hadn't told anyone, not even Maggie, about my encounter with my mother, but I figured Dad had the right to know.

"Dad, something very strange occurred while I was in the coma. I saw and spoke to Mom."

"You --- you saw your mother? How?"

"I have no idea how. I just know that I did and she was as real as you are right now."

"Was she --- happy?"

"Yes, very much so, and she asked me to give you a message."

Dad watched me expectantly.

"She wanted you to know that whatever happened between the two of you, she forgives you and she wants you to be happy too. You and Bernice have her blessing."

Dad crumbled.

He put his head in his arms on the side of my bed and wept.

"I never meant to hurt her --- not on purpose. I loved her, but I was just a dumb shit with my head up my ass. I have wished a thousand times that I could do it all over --- for her and for you."

"She wanted to lift that burden off your shoulders and give you peace."

"Thank you," he said. "Thank you both."

I had never really seen the true power of forgiveness, but after watching my dad that day, I figured that maybe the Big Guy had things pretty well under control after all.

Dad, Bernice, Willie, Mary and Jerry couldn't stay away.

The guests kept coming and finally, Nurse Ratchett had had enough.

If this gal hadn't been a nurse, she probably could have been a linebacker with the Kansas City Chiefs. Her arms were about the size of my legs. She had the demeanor of a linebacker as well.

"Okay, all of you, clear out! I've got work to do here."

My friends stared in amazement.

When no one moved, she raised her voice an octave. "Maybe I didn't make myself clear. Why don't you folks go to the cafeteria and get a snack. I need to check Mr. Williams. You can come back when I'm finished."

On the way out of the door, Jerry quipped, "Walt, maybe you can save her some time. If she needs samples of your urine, blood, semen, and stool, you can just give her your underwear."

Dad chuckled, and Nurse Ratchett glared as they filed out of the door.

Things were going better than I had hoped for. She checked my blood pressure, took my temperature, and listened to my heart. As she was packing away her goodies, I rose up and swung my feet over the edge of the bed.

"Where do you think you're going?"

"To the bathroom."

"Nope. Your chart says you might possibly have internal injuries, so you have to stay down until the doctor runs some tests."

"But I have to—uh—you know."

"Then you're going to have to—uh—you know in this." She pulled a bedpan off the closet shelf.

I looked at the plastic contraption. I'd seen them before, but I'd never used one. "Look, I'm fine. There's nothing wrong with me. I can certainly walk to the bathroom."

Then she got that look that I'd once seen in the eyes of Mean Joe Green.

"You're fine when we say you're fine. Do you understand? Now get your feet back in that bed." She plopped the bedpan in my lap.

When I didn't respond, she gave me the look again. "Well?"

"Well, I'm not going to use this thing with you standing there watching me. I'd like some privacy."

She shook her head and started for the door.

"Oh, say, I haven't eaten since lunch yesterday. Am I permitted to have breakfast?"

She picked up my chart again. "I'll see what I can do."

When she was gone, I picked up the bedpan. The first thing I noticed was that it was cold. Brrr. I turned the thing over, hoping that instructions would be printed on the backside, but there were none. With my luck, they would have probably been written in Chinese anyway.

They must figure that everyone instinctually knows how to use one of these things. Like it's something innate that's passed down through our DNA. If so, there were definitely some deficiencies in my gene pool. So do you lie down on the thing? I tried it and nearly broke my back.

So you sit on it. Do your legs stick out in front of you on the bed, or do you turn it sideways and let your legs dangle over the edge?

I tried it both ways, and the only way that it was comfortable was to dangle my feet over the edge.

By the time I had turned it and climbed on top, I had exerted more energy than just padding the six steps to the bathroom.

So there I sat, perched on my plastic throne, and to my dismay, nothing happened. It was obvious that my bowels were balking. I was tempted to just chuck the whole thing and march over to the real toilet, but to be quite truthful, I was scared of Nurse Ratchett.

Then I saw it, and an idea formed in my head. On the little table next to my bed was a box full of rubber gloves. Normally, I hate seeing those because it usually means that someone is going to be sticking something somewhere I don't want it stuck.

I grabbed a pair of the gloves, slipped them on, and put my ear to the door listening for footsteps. Hearing none, I slipped into the bathroom and did my job the way it's supposed to be done. Fortunately, the resulting deposit was solid and a floater.

I reached in with my gloved hand, scooped up what was left of yesterday's lunch, and plopped it in the bedpan. Nurse Ratchett would never notice the difference.

Being a cop, I realized that if I was going to commit the perfect crime, I would have to destroy the evidence.

I peeled off the gloves and was about to throw them in the wastebasket but checked myself. She might see them there. I looked at the stool. If it could handle some of the stuff I've deposited over the years, surely it could handle two little latex gloves.

What I hadn't thought of was that these little gloves, unlike my previous deposits, had fingers. Evidently, one or more of those little fingers had clutched the innards of the stool, and I watched in horror as the water, instead of circling and disappearing, steadily rose to the top of the bowl.

"No! No! Nooo!"

I heaved a sigh of relief when I heard the water stop. Another drop would have put it over the edge.

I looked around and saw a plunger in the corner. I grabbed it and slipped it into the water. Of course the Law of Archimedes took over, and the water displaced by the plunger overflowed into the floor.

The waves caused by my plunging sent more cascades over the edge, and by the time the gloves had been dislodged, there was a mess to clean up.

I grabbed a towel and was on my hands and knees mopping up water with my ass hanging out of the stupid hospital gown when I heard, "Mr. Williams!"

I looked up, and Nurse Ratchett was staring at my bare behind. I cringed, expecting a tirade that would make a sailor blush, but instead her attention had been directed to my little gift in the bedpan.

She just had a bewildered look on her face. "I've been a nurse for twenty-seven years, but this is a new one." She got me a clean gown and fresh towels, and I climbed back in bed.

By this time she had regained her composure.

"Apparently you have difficulty following orders, and you definitely have authority issues."

I was about to argue, but I figured I'd better just clam up. As they say, there's no such thing as a perfect crime.

"Mr. Williams, you *have* to stay in bed until after your tests."

"Yes, ma'am."

She emptied the bedpan, rinsed, and flushed. She returned with the bedpan and a gizmo that looked like the thing my mechanic uses to put oil in my car. "Now, if you have to urinate or defecate, please use these."

She had said please, but the tone in her voice said, "Do it or else." Just then the door opened, and an orderly brought in a tray.

"I ordered you some breakfast."

The orderly set the tray on my bed table. I was starving, and all during my bathroom escapade I had been envisioning eggs, toast, bacon, maybe even a pancake. I was shocked to see a pile of quivering green stuff, a bowl of yellow swill, and a cup of something barely darker than water.

"What's this?"

"Your breakfast, of course. Lime Jell-O, broth, and tea."

"Don't I even get toast?"

"No, Mr. Williams, you're on a liquid diet until after your tests. Bon appétit." I know she was grinning when she walked out the door.

I looked at my breakfast. I like Jell-O. I just don't like green Jell-O. I know they make Jell-O in other colors. I've seen it. Green just isn't my favorite color. I've tried green shampoo, but I like white better. I love a red, ripe tomato, but I just can't do a green one. I absolutely hate the green stuff that grows on your food when you leave it in the fridge too long.

I was perilously close to digging into my liquid breakfast when my friends returned.

Dad looked at the pitiful pile of glop on my tray. "I thought so. I've been where you are before. Bet you're hungry, aren't you?"

I nodded my head.

"Willie, watch the door."

Dad reached into a sack and pulled out one of those fluffy, golden brown biscuits with egg, cheese, and bacon.

I almost cried. "I love you, Dad." It just came out, and it surprised both of us.

Maggie almost came unglued. "Dad! How could you? The hospital has rules…and the tests… Walt has tests to take…and…"

"Tests, shmefts. The kid's fit as a fiddle. And look at that swill they gave him to eat. If he wasn't sick before, he sure would be after he ate that."

He looked at Bernice for approval, and she obligingly nodded her head.

Maggie turned to Jerry and the professor for support, but they just shrugged their shoulders.

"You're all incorrigible," she muttered.

After I wolfed down the biscuit and Dad tucked the wrappers away in his pocket, I had an idea.

"Dad, before you leave, could you go to a vending machine and bring me a Mountain Dew?"

"Sure, sonny. Be right back."

I had just stashed my Dew under my mattress when Nurse Ratchett returned.

"You folks have to leave. It's time for Mr. Williams's tests."

We said our good-byes, and as everyone was leaving, the professor, who had been unusually quiet, turned to speak. I was expecting some words of wisdom or comfort from the old man.

"Walt, I hope your tests come out better than those of a friend of mine."

"Oh really?"

"Yes, he went to the doctor with a sprig of greenery sticking out of his bottom. He said, 'Doc, I think I have lettuce growing out of my rear end.' The doctor examined the greenery and said, 'I'm afraid I have some bad news—that's only the tip of the iceberg.'"

Without another word, he turned and left, leaving me with my mouth hanging open. The professor was obviously spending too much time with Jerry.

My tests went well, and the doctor proclaimed me fit to resume my normal activities. I returned to my room and started preparing my parting gift to Nurse Ratchett.

I dug the Mountain Dew from under my mattress, popped the top, poured it into the funny little beaker she had given me, and placed it on the bed table.

I had just finished when Nurse Ratchett popped in.

"I'm going off duty in ten minutes. I just wanted to check and see if you needed anything before I left."

"Why thank you. Here, you might want to get rid of this." I picked up the beaker of yellow liquid and started to hand it to her, but instead I brought it back and chugged every last drop.

Nurse Ratchett blanched, gasped, "Oh my God!" and fainted dead away.

I called Maggie and gave her the good news that I was free at last and she could pick me up at any time.

She was devastated that she was tied up with clients all day.

I told her not to worry. I would call Ox. He would get me home and I would see her later.

I made the call and was about to change from that disgusting gown into my civvies, when Agent Blackburn walked into the room.

"Hey, Walt. Sorry I haven't been here to see you sooner. The brass has kept me pretty tied up with the elderberry thing. We're making some progress. We've got some of the corporate fat cats and shady politicians shaking in their boots."

"Good to hear," I said. "I suppose you know that they were the ones who had me tossed off the roof."

"I did know that and we've been trying to get a lead on those two, but they've gone underground."

Then I remembered what my mother had said.

"You do realize that they're probably after you too."

"As soon as we heard about the attempt on your life, the Bureau assigned teams to watch my back around the clock. There's been no sign of anyone."

"So where are your guys now?" I asked, looking around.

"They're taking a break. We figured I'd be safe in the hospital. They'll pick me up outside."

"Well, you watch your back. I've been released and Ox will be here in a few minutes to take me home."

"Then I'll get out of your hair. As always, it was a pleasure doing business with you. Maybe we can do it again some day."

"Sure. Anytime you need an old guy, just give me a call."

He laughed and waved and was on his way.

I watched him leave and as soon as he was out of my door, two men in lab coats walked up on either side of him.

I saw one of them press something into his back and whisper in his ear.

The other turned and glanced down the hall.

I saw his face and recognized him as one of the goons who had given me flying lessons.

Blackburn was being abducted and his backup was nowhere in sight.

At that moment Ox walked in the door.

"Hey partner. Are you ready to make like a hockey player and get the puck out of here?"

"Ox," I said pointing, "that's Agent Blackburn and he's being abducted. I think they have a gun in his back.

"OK," he said. "Let's figure this out."

Just then, a portly orderly was wheeling an empty gurney down the hall.

"Quick," I said, "give me your badge and your gun."

Ox handed them over and I flagged down the orderly.

I showed him the badge.

"Kansas City Police. We need your gurney and your scrubs --- NOW!"

The orderly stripped and I tossed the scrubs to Ox. "Put these on. Quick!"

He slipped on the scrubs and I crawled under the sheet on the gurney.

"This hallway is a big circle. Go the opposite of the way they took Blackburn and we'll cut them off before they reach the elevator. Step on it!"

Ox barreled down the hallway dodging doctors, patients and nurses.

He swerved around the first corner and almost took out an old guy pushing his saline rack.

We rounded the second corner and saw Blackburn and the two goons heading our way.

As we approached, I sat up on the gurney and caught Blackburn's eye.

He recognized us and nodded.

When we were just a few feet from the trio, I threw back the sheet and leveled Ox's pistol at one of the goons.

"Kansas City Police. Drop your gun and put your hands in the air."

Blackburn did one of those fancy twisty turns that they teach you at Quantico and had the guy with the gun on the floor.

The second guy turned to run, but Ox was on him in a flash.

After they were both in cuffs, one of them gave me a close look.

"I thought you was dead!"

"Yea," I said. "I've been getting that a lot lately. Maybe someday, but not today."

# CHAPTER 35

My hospital release was delayed by the debriefing and paperwork involved with the two assassins.

But finally, everything was wrapped up and Ox drove me home.

Everyone in the building wanted to throw another 'Welcome Home Walt' party, but Maggie had persuaded them to give it a rest and let me settle in peacefully.

We enjoyed a leisurely supper and Maggie caught me up on her activities while I had been hospitalized.

Toward the end of the evening, Maggie inquired as to whether my body had recuperated sufficiently to engage in some activities of a more intimate nature.

I did a quick check and determined that I was fit to go.

Maggie slipped into that little black nightie with the fur around the edges that barely covered her --- well, it barely covered it.

My first encounter with this garment was on our honeymoon and Maggie had worn it infrequently since then, usually only on special occasions.

I sensed that she had planned the evening ahead of time and that she considered her husband's return from oblivion, a special occasion.

When we hit the sheets, I could tell that Maggie was ready to go and so was I --- but Mr. Winkie was a no-show.

After a while, Maggie sensed that something was definitely wrong.

"Walt, are you OK. You're usually --- uhhh --- more enthusiastic."

It certainly wasn't a lack of enthusiasm. Maggie had certainly done her best to whet my appetite, but something was holding me back.

Then it occurred to me; I remembered Mom's comment, "Based on what I've seen, you and Maggie are doing everything just right."

It was the 'everything' that had sent Mr. Winkie into hiding.

Somehow a man can't do his best work if he thinks his mom might be in the room watching.

I hadn't told Maggie about my experience while in the coma, and I figured this might be a good time.

I certainly didn't want her to think that my lack of responsiveness reflected on her in any way.

We spent the next hour talking about the visit with my mom.

I have to give Maggie credit; such a far-fetched story could have been met with skepticism and doubt, but Maggie was totally supportive.

When our discussion of things ethereal had concluded, Maggie looked around the bedroom.

"I have a theory. I'm betting that spirits can't see in the dark any better than we can. Shall we give it a try?"

I turned off the light and crawled into bed next to my sweetie.

In the total darkness of the room, Mr. Winkie suddenly appeared. Maybe Maggie was right.

Later, as I lay back, exhausted, another one of those weird things that inhabit the deep recesses of my brain popped into my mind.

I remembered, as a kid, seeing Jimmy Durante, the comedian, on TV.

After every performance, he would sign off with the words, "Goodnight Mrs. Calabash, wherever you are."

I thought about my mom and how much I missed her and my last words before dropping off to sleep were, "Goodnight Mrs. Williams, wherever you are."

$$R_x$$

Try as I might, I couldn't get my out-of-body experience out of my mind.

I needed to talk to someone with some insight into things beyond the realm of normal human experience.

My first thought was Pastor Bob, but I already knew what his response would be.

It was a foregone conclusion that he believed in something beyond the decay of our mortal flesh.

It was his Boss who had uttered the words that had brought comfort to the multitudes over the centuries, *"In my Father's house are many mansions. If it were not so, I would have told you. I go to prepare a place for you."*

I had always been willing to go with that, simply because the alternative, that there is nothing more and than we are no different than road kill rotting on the highway, is totally unacceptable.

But I wanted a more analytic approach, not based on religious dogma.

The obvious choice was the Professor.

With a Doctorate in Philosophy and years of academic teaching, I thought he might have some valuable insights into my experience.

He listened quietly as I related my incredible story.

When I finished, I simply asked, "Was it real or was I dreaming?"

"I wish that the answer was that simple. The first question on which everything else is based is if there is life after death.

"Life after death can neither be proved nor disproved. This is because one would have to undergo physical death in order to prove or disprove it, and, by its very nature, disproving it would not be possible.

"One either believes or disbelieves and that is the basis of faith."

"Very well then," I said, "let's go with the premise that there is something beyond the grave. How does my experience fit into that scenario?"

"Then it puts you in with a very elite group of individuals. You had what has been called an NDE, a near-death experience, and an OBE, an out-of-body experience. It is estimated that eighteen percent of individuals who had been resuscitated from cardiac arrest have reported the same kind of experience."

"But don't critics explain that away by attributing such phenomena to complex defense mechanisms of a dying brain?"

"That's certainly one explanation. The human brain is the most complex and least understood thing in our known universe.

"As your hero, Dirty Harry, likes to say, "Opinions are like assholes; everybody has one." Well brains are like assholes too. Everyone has one, but no one really understands what it is capable of."

"So are you saying that what I experienced was nothing more than screwed up neurons firing away in my cerebral cortex?"

"Quite the contrary. In 1991 in Atlanta, Georgia, Pam Reynolds had a near-death experience. Reynolds underwent surgery for a brain aneurysm, and the procedure required doctors to drain all the blood from her brain. The woman was kept literally brain-dead by the surgical team for a full 45 minutes. Despite being clinically dead, when Reynolds was resuscitated, she described some amazing things. She recounted experiences she had while dead -- like interacting with deceased relatives. Even more amazing is that Reynolds was able to describe aspects of the surgical procedure, down to the bone saw that was used to remove part of her skull."

"So what does that prove?"

"It doesn't 'prove' anything, but a brain-dead person should not be able to form new memories -- he shouldn't have any consciousness at all, really. So how can anything but a metaphysical explanation account for her experience?"

"So are you saying that what I experienced was real?"

"Was it real to you?"

"As real as me sitting here with you right now."

"And how did your experience make you feel?'

"It was one of the most beautiful and comforting experiences in my entire life."

"Then that's all that really matters, isn't it?"

After I left, I realized that the Professor had left me exactly as had Pastor Bob.

I had gone looking for answers.

True or not true?

Real or a figment of my imagination?

But instead, he had made me look deep within, and decide for myself.

I wonder who teaches these guys to do that?

# EPILOGUE

The capture of the two men that had tried to bring my law enforcement career to an end, along with our elderberry caper, focused new attention on the collusion between greedy corporate executives and corrupt public officials.

While our form of government is head and shoulders above any other, its success or failure is determined by the moral character of those elected to represent us.

When, out of greed and the lust for power, the public trust is violated by the wolves in sheep's clothing, the very fabric of our society is put at risk.

Often, the battle against the rich and powerful seems futile and it is much easier to just look the other way, but sometimes the mighty are brought to their knees by the seemingly insignificant.

The classic illustration of that principle is H.G. Well's novel, *War Of The Worlds*.

The story is of a Martian invasion of the earth. Human weapons had proven useless against the powerful invaders and just when it appeared that all was lost, the Martians fell to microscopic bacteria to which humans were immune.

One can only hope that maybe something so simple as an elderberry could be the catalyst that initiates the reform that will bring an end to the corruption and collusion that put our way of life at risk.

One thing that recent events made perfectly clear to me was that as individuals and families, we have choices.

I discovered that it is never too late to find a new passion that makes life worth living.

I found that it is never too late to find someone to love and share your life with.

I learned from Dr. Pearson that our bodies are a wonder of creation and perfectly capable of maintaining themselves with proper care and nutrition.

We can choose to pollute our bodies with Big Macs, Krispy Kremes, meat laced with growth hormones and vegetables sprayed with pesticides, or we can take the time, effort and expense to choose healthy, organic foods that will give our bodies the essentials to be strong and vibrant.

We can fall prey to the constant barrage of ads on TV and in our newspapers paid for by pharmaceutical giants telling us to 'ask your doctor if Drug X is right for you', or we can seek the counsel of health practitioners trained to offer us alternatives to the devastating side effects of commercial drug products.

We can bury our heads in the sand and let the collusion of the powerful pharmaceutical giants and the corrupt politicians exist as 'business as usual', or we can stand together and say, "We're mad as hell and we're not going to tolerate this anymore!"

Life is about making choices, for ourselves, our family and our way of life.

Choose wisely!

# TESTIMONIAL

### *Robert & Peg Thornhill*

In 2007, my wife, Peg, and I moved back to Missouri from Maui where we had spent the last five years.

We moved to a log home on seventy acres just outside of Osceola, Mo., a town of 835 residents.

After five years of island food, we had now moved into a town where the only restaurant served heaping piles of deep-fried chicken, mashed potatoes covered with gravy and home-made yeast rolls.

We discovered, to our dismay, that at the age of sixty-four our metabolism had slowed down, we had gained weight and we felt sluggish.

One of our reasons for moving back to Missouri was to be close to our children and grandson.

Peg's son, Dr. Britt Batchelor and his wife Wendy were in their middle-age years and, like us, while by no means obese, had begun to plump up.

On one of our visits, after having not seen them for several weeks, we were shocked to see that both of them were lean and trim and had a whole new outlook on life.

Naturally, we were both curious and impressed as to what they were doing.

They shared with us that they had met Dr. Edward Pearson through a professional organization to which they both belonged, and that they were participating in the Detoxification Program of his New Medicine Foundation.

We pressed them for details of what they were doing and were so impressed with their results, we asked Britt to introduce us to Dr. Pearson.

Thus began a relationship that has changed our lives.

Coincidentally, we had been referred to a book entitled, Natural Cures "They" Don't Want You To Know About, by Kevin Trudeau.

From reading the material sent to us by Dr. Pearson and the Trudeau book, we soon discovered that what we were about to undertake was not just another 'fad diet' like you find in the women's magazines at the grocery counter, but rather involved a complete life-style change.

We learned that after sixty-four years of eating whatever, whenever and where ever, our bodies were filled with toxins not only from the environment, but more importantly, from the chemical additives, growth hormones, antibiotics and insecticides that were packed into what we eat by the food industry.

After studying the material, our first task was to flush the built-up toxins from our bodies using Dr. Pearson's protocols.

And yes, like Walt in the story you just read, it involved the dreaded colon cleanse. And yes, many of Walt's adventures and misadventures as Maggie led him into a healthier life-style, were written from my own perspective as one who has traveled this road.

We continued to study as we progressed through the 'detox' phase and came to realize that if we wanted to keep our bodies strong and healthy that this was just the first step and in many ways, the easiest step.

After a few weeks the 'detox' phase would be over, but we learned that if it were to have any lasting effect, we would need to make some drastic changes that would last the rest of our lives.

The whole fabric of our society is centered around food and drink.

Family affairs, social occasions and nights out are celebrated around the meal.

Our shopping habits have been engrained in us over the years and as we move down the grocery aisle, we mindlessly pluck the same products from the shelf that we have been buying for years.

Changing those engrained habits was one of the most difficult tasks.

Once we learned that the vast majority of the foods we eat are filled with chemicals that prolong shelf life and contain substances that are as dangerous and as addictive as the nicotine in cigarettes, it meant shopping in a different way.

We began by looking at the labels of the food we had been purchasing and realized that they were filled with high fructose corn syrup, hydrogenated corn oil and artificial sweeteners, all poisons to the human body.

We discovered that in order to get the meat from the stock pens to the grocer faster, the corporate farms had pumped the animals full of growth hormones and antibiotics.

It took awhile, but we finally found stores where we could purchase organic food that was grown naturally and free of the poisons introduced by the huge corporations to generate higher profits.

A major life-style change is never easy.

Nothing worthwhile in life usually is.

It probably took the better part of six months to go through our detox and change our eating and shopping habits.

At the end of that time Peg and I had flushed the built-up toxins from our bodies, lowered our cholesterol and had each dropped thirty pounds.

We both felt better than we had in years and were determined to stay on the path to better health.

Was it easy? No!

Was it worthwhile? Definitely!

After reading this, one might wonder if our new lifestyle was like that of the monks locked away in a monastery eating only that which they grew.

Far from it.

While there were major changes, such as not consuming the case of Sprite each week as we had done previously and cutting back on the deep fried chicken at the Bus Stop Cafe, we found that the world was full of wonderful meals made from nutritious ingredients.

If there was anything negative in our experience, it was the reaction of some of our friends, family and acquaintances.

Many had the same reaction as we did when we saw Britt and Wendy's results and, of course, everyone wanted to know what we had done.

Most of those with whom we shared our experience were just not ready for such a drastic lifestyle change.

We heard excuses such as "Organic food costs too much. I can't afford it."

It's true. A bag of regular carrots costs ninety-nine cents while a bad of organic carrots costs a buck and a half.

Yet, these same people spend $200.00 on a prescription because they're sick all the time.

We would rather spend the extra fifty cents on the organic food than a whole lot more for drugs.

Everything in life is about choices.

Sometimes the choices are deliberate, but many times our choices are made by taking no action at all.

Living a healthy lifestyle is definitely a deliberate choice.

As Confucius said, "A journey of a thousand miles begins with the first step."

Like Walt and Maggie, Peg and I have taken that step and hope you are encouraged to do the same.

# ABOUT THE AUTHOR

Robert Thornhill began writing at the age of sixty-six, and in two short years has penned six novels in the Lady Justice mystery/comedy series, the seven volume Rainbow Road series of chapter books for children, a cookbook and a mini-autobiography.

Robert's latest novel in his Lady Justice series, Lady Justice And Dr. Death was chosen as the Pinnacle Book Achievement Award winner as the best mystery novel for fall of 2011 by the North American Bookdealers Exchange.

Robert holds a master's degree in psychology, but his wit and insight come from his varied occupations including thirty years as a real estate broker.

He lives with his wife, Peg, in Independence, Mo.

Visit him on the Web at: http://BooksByBob.com

### Note To Reader

In August of 2011, I completed the fifth novel in the Lady Justice mystery/comedy series, *Lady Justice And The Sting*.

As I always do, I sent copies of the completed manuscript to several friends and acquaintances for their feedback and comments before sending the manuscript to the publisher.

Since the plot involved a holistic physician, I sent a copy to Dr. Edward Pearson in Florida.

Dr. Pearson loved the premise of the book and the style of writing, particularly as it related to alternative healthcare, natural products and Walt's transformation into a healthier lifestyle.

In subsequent conversations, Dr. Pearson shared that he had been looking for a book that he could share with his patients, colleagues and peers that would spread his message in a format that would capture their imagination and their hearts.

*The Sting* was very close to what he had been looking for and he made the suggestion that maybe we could work together to produce just the right book.

Using *The Sting* as the basis of the new book, I added Walt's various adventures and misadventures with doctors, hospitals and health care in general and *Wolves In Sheep's Clothing* was born.

I hope you enjoyed it and more importantly, I hope you took to heart the message it was meant to deliver.

If Walt, Maggie, Mary, Willie and the rest of the gang brought a smile to your face, I hope you will get to know them better in the Lady Justice novels on the following pages.

Robert Thornhill, Author

### *LADY JUSTICE TAKES A C.R.A.P.*

City Retiree Action Patrol

This is where it all began.

See how sixty-five year old Walt Williams became a cop and started the City Retiree Action Patrol. Meet Maggie, Willie, Mary and the Professor, Walt's sidekicks in all the Lady Justice novels. Laugh out loud as Walt and his band of Senior Scrappers capture the 'Realtor Rapist' and take down the 'Russian Mob'

### *LADY JUSTICE AND THE LOST TAPES*

In Lady Justice and the Lost Tapes, Walt and his band of scrappy seniors continue their battle against the forces of evil. When an entire Eastside Kansas City neighborhood is terrorized by the mob, Walt must go undercover to help solve the case. Later, the amazing discovery of a previously unknown recording session by a deceased rock 'n' roll idol stuns the music industry.

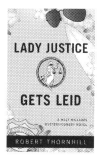

### *LADY JUSTICE GETS LEI'D*

In Lady Justice Gets Lei'd, Walt and Maggie plan a romantic honeymoon on the beautiful Hawaiian islands, but ancient artifacts discovered in a cave in a dormant volcano and a surprising revelation about Maggie's past, lead our lovers into the hands of Hawaiian zealots

### *LADY JUSTICE AND THE AVENGING ANGELS*

Lady Justice has unwittingly entered a religious war. Who better to fight for her than Walt Williams? The Avenging Angels believe it's their job to rain fire and brimstone on Kansas City, their Sodom and Gomorrah.In this compelling addition to the Lady Justice series, Robert Thornhill brings back all the characters readers have come to love for more hilarity and higher stakes. You'll laugh, and you'll be on the edge of your seat until the big finish. Don't miss Lady Justice and the Avenging Angels!

## LADY JUSTICE AND THE STING

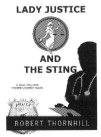

In Lady Justice and The Sting, a holistic physician is murdered and Walt becomes entangled in the high-powered world of pharmaceutical giants and corrupt politicians. Maggie, Ox, Willie, Mary and all your favorite characters are back to help Walt bring the criminals to justice in the most unorthodox ways. A dead-serious mystery with hilarious twists!

## LADY JUSTICE AND DR. DEATH

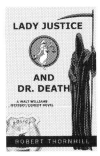

In Lady Justice and Dr. Death, a series of terminally ill patients are found dead under circumstances that point to a new Dr. Death practicing euthanasia in the Kansas City area.

Walt and his entourage of scrappy seniors are dragged into the 'right-to-die with dignity' controversy.

The mystery provides a light-hearted look at this explosive topic and death in general.

You may see end-of-life issues in a whole new light after reading Lady Justice and Dr. Death.

***RAINBOW ROAD***
CHAPTER BOOKS FOR CHILDREN
AGES 5 – 10

Super Secrets Of Rainbow Road
Super Powers Of Rainbow Road
Hawaiian Rainbows
Patriotic Rainbows
Sports Heroes Of Rainbow Road
Ghosts And Goblins Of Rainbow Road
Christmas Crooks Of Rainbow Road

For more information, please go to
**http://www.BooksByBob.com**